A Souvenir from Qam

Holt, Rinehart and Winston
New York   Chicago   San Francisco

A Souvenir from

QAM

by Marc Connelly

Copyright © 1965 by Marc Connelly

Published simultaneously in Canada by Holt, Rinehart and Winston of Canada, Limited.

Library of Congress Catalog Card Number: 65-10126

Published, May, 1965
Second Printing, May, 1965

Designer: Ernst Reichl
81534-0315
Printed in the United States of America

A Souvenir from Qam

Chapter 1

The road was about to dip again and turn south. Newton Bemis stopped the car for a final look behind him. Through the mist of new leaves on the maples the roof of the house could still be seen. A handkerchief of smoke waved good-bye from one of the stone chimneys. Newton was tempted to wave back. After a moment he faced forward and pressed the ignition button.

It was one-thirty. With little traffic he could be back in New York in time for handball before dinner. He hoped there would be no more idiotic deference in the locker room because of that embarrassing piece in *Short*. When its flirtatious reporter had begun spouting compliments even before she sat down, he should have scented trouble. How could Mr. Thackaray have permitted such stupid exploitation of a busy employee?

Bursts of flowering dogwood and fragrance from a roadside orchard requickened his awareness of the vernal excitement about him. In the early warmth of May, Vermont was hastening to dress for its wedding with June. This was not a time to flagellate oneself with annoyances. Before the summer was gone the alterations would be completed and the lovely old Elkins house would be his to live in, and, if not a cure for all ills, at least an anodyne of comfort and relaxation. Even arranging the mortgage had been painless, pleasant in fact, because of the solvency assured by his new contract. A month ago his morbid fear of debt would have made the encumbrance of a mortgage unbearable.

It was almost dizzying to consider the blessings before him. Luxuries such as windows that faced north, south, east, and west; windows unsealed by air conditioners; windows that could be opened and closed, through which one could watch the seasons re-embrace the compliant hills. The commodious study converted from the "family" parlor would be pleasantly dusky on bright days because of the copper beech that guarded that corner of the house from wind and sun. The ceiling of the study would not be much higher than the one in New York, but there would be no harassing cross fire of noises. Above all, he had a dwelling place in which a family could grow.

He was glad that he had decided to wait until he was thirty before again considering marriage. He was no longer the rash suitor of six years ago. This time, if he should find a likely candidate, the possibility of marriage would be considered wisely, less conditioned by youthful emotions and appetites. Here, the drowsing Attendant Realist within him became wakeful. *You think you're wise now?*

Of course I'm not. Ask me when I'm sixty. Right now, leave me alone. Hell, of course, he would never be truly wise. But now he could surely rely more on his judgment.

A cloud of apple blossoms bending over a rail fence almost touched his head. With a deep breath he drank in the budding world about him. Could one sail any closer to the shores of bliss? The long weekend spent in acquiring the property had been pure delight. How fortunate that he had found Mr. Elkins still there. Another week and he'd have left to spend his remaining years with his grandchildren in California. Mr. Elkins had remembered Newton's father and seemed pleased that his ancestral home, still "right as a trivet" after two hundred years of use, wouldn't go to a complete stranger. He hoped his staff of a house-keeper-cook, gardener-caretaker, and a maid-of-all-work would fill Newton's needs.

"They're all fine people. I promised I'd try to get them more money but even with the raises they won't set you back more than six hundred a month."

It was pleasant to hear phrases like "set you back" in an age of comptometers.

"You won't get your roses until the end of June, but you can see how big the bushes are. Since Mis' Elkins died we haven't used the hothouse for much besides starting seedlings but the pipes work and all the frames are intact. Like to go bobsleddin'? Half that hill's yours and the Harpers have always been happy to have young people start down from the crest on their property. There's three or four sleds down in the playhouse. One of them is an eight-seater."

And glimpsing old Charlie Brewer had been refreshing, too. When Mr. Brewer had been postmaster, if you asked him how he felt he would say without pausing for breath, "Newty, I'm finer than frog's hair fit as a fiddle chuck full o' buckwheat ready to fight fires all day and how's your good self?" If Mr. Brewer had not been dozing on his porch it would have been good to say hello. He could do it when he came up again next month. It would be good, too, to hear Mr. Brewer again dramatically interject his, "Well, thinks I," in recounting his experiences.

Wasn't the village ahead where Rudyard Kipling had lived while writing the Jungle Books? What was the name of the Vermont girl he had married? Ballinger? No—Balestier. Caroline Starr Balestier. Being so exuberant made one forgetful.

How would the psychometrists from the Noonan Clinic rate his McLandress Dimension Coefficient—his "Macelsee," the interviewer has called it—today? "We are determining how long subjects' thoughts can remain centered on substantive phenomena other than their own personalities." What a joke on skeptics like himself if those concentration quotients proved valid. The bland defensiveness of the Noonan man recalled Faraday's poser to the woman who asked what earthly use there could be in his inductor. "Madam, what good is a baby?" Why did so many outstanding individuals have ratings of less than five minutes? Of course it had been infantile to be so pleased, but interesting nonetheless, to learn his own was exactly that of Dr. Robert Oppenheimer.

Against the tide of northbound traffic Newton sped down Riverside Drive turning east on 79th Street. Southbound on Broadway a traffic light stopped him beside a newsstand. Tacked to the side facing him, an advertising placard blazed: "Like to know your future? Read this month's *Short.*" Goddamn it, here he was plunged again into the world of frivolous questions and answers. It was comforting to know that tomorrow he would again find sanctuary in that fortress of sanity only science invited one to enter.

Webster Harris appeared enthralled as the wife of the head of the Chilean financial mission predicted fine early skiing at Legunillas and Farellones, his vague smile and averted eyes implying rapturous envisionment of the Andes in June. Actually he was again appreciating the loveliness of Rowena McGravey which he had not been able to do for several minutes. Now she and the French press attaché were coming back into the room.

The press attaché halted a circulating waiter. Rowena accepted a glass of champagne and sipped it. This was odd; Rowena disliked champagne. Tony Quilling, the British First, joined them and Rowena and Quilling moved away from the congestion in the middle of the room and were engrossed in conversation when the new Dutch military aide swooped down on them. Apparently he was being amusing. Rowena laughed in a wintry way and looked about her. When her eyes met Webster's her left hand darted above her head and her fingers fluttered playfully, her signal that she wanted to leave. This, too, was odd. Rowena had never left a cocktail party this early.

Webster deplored his inability to come to Chile during the snow season and got away. Rowena had already started for the door. He caught up with her a few feet from where the chargé d'affaires and his wife were still greeting guests. Rowena's good-byes were convincingly bright and chatty, but she got into Webster's car without murmuring her customary thanks to Webster's driver for opening the door.

Webster was discreetly silent until the embassy was two blocks behind them. Then he pressed the knob of the window-control panel to insure privacy. Rowena did not respond immediately to the invitation of the ascended glass. She was ransacking her purse and her memory.

"I have no cigarettes."

Webster produced one and flicked his lighter. Simultaneously a recollection ignited in Rowena. *Of course! The only possible explanation was Claudie Bracque.* The weight on her heart lessened a bit.

"Do you know Claudie Bracque, Webster?"

"I don't think so. A relative of the painter?"

"No. She spells it with a 'c'. Her husband publishes *Le Monde du Chic*. The new press attaché thought I'd like to see next month's issue. Claudie must have believed I was trying to steal Enzo Barelli last summer at Porto Santo Stefano."

"Enzo Barelli! I've heard that name, but—"

"He's a movie actor. And part faun. I had trouble convincing him I was not an available nymph. I remember someone telling me he was Claudie's property. Fancy her smoldering this long."

"Go ahead, dear."

"It's one of those 'Ten Most Beautiful Women' things. This time they've picked Washington." There was the slightest pause. "And I am Number Seven."

Webster recognized sportsmanship in the little laugh.

"The pictures of the first six have a full page each. I've been slapped on a page in the back with the last three." She studied the tiny smudge of lipstick at the tip of her cigarette. "Do you think I'm a vain girl, Webster?"

"Certainly not. You happen to be incredibly beautiful and you have every right to recognize the fact." The unassailable logic of his statement seemed to comfort her somewhat.

"I suppose the first four could be explained on the grounds of diplomatic courtesy. They are all embassy women. But the fifth and sixth!"

"Who are they?"

"Congresswomen." Webster stared.

"Rowena!"

"Seriously. Two congresswomen. Then gruesome me."

His professional training helped Webster curb his indignation. He recalled the looks of current female Representatives. Some were rather attractive. But to compare any woman to Rowena! Discipline could not silence him completely.

"I can't believe it!"

Rowena turned to him. Webster was really sweet. Why couldn't he be as physically magnetic as Tony Quilling? It would make life so much easier. Papa said Webster might be well on his way to top diplomatic posts. And it was conceivable that with effort he might be made less of an altar boy. She patted the hand he had placed on hers.

"Let's not think about it any more, dear. Actually it's quite amusing. Claudie Bracque rather surprised me, that's all." This time her laugh seemed perfectly natural.

Rowena closed her eyes and leaned toward her comforter. In Georgetown Bates stopped before her house on N Street. Rowena told Webster he could pick her up at eight-thirty for the Brazilian Ambassador's dinner and waved him happily on his way.

Webster was no more a simpleton than many men in love. When not worshipping Rowena, he was as bright a junior official as you could find in the Protocol Bureau.

Even before entering Harvard Law School he had decided upon a career in diplomacy. Shortly after joining the State Department he had won an assignment to the Blood Bank, that pool of young men available to qualified Washington hostesses when stricken by last minute defections among their dinner guests. In less than five years his competence had advanced him to his present echelon, the Riot Squad, whose members are prepared for instant dispatch to any foreign posts where social *gaffes* by government representatives or their wives require immediate remedy.

Webster had met Rowena two years ago at a White House reception. She had recently come to the capital with her father, the newly-elected Senator Clovis McGravey. Then twenty-eight and serenely radiant, Rowena had dazzled Webster when they met. Before the evening was gone Webster knew he had found his ideal woman. Rowena, more equipped to receive admiration than bestow it, found Webster pleasant and undemanding. Later that night, exhilarated by her introduction to Washington society, Rowena lay in bed wide awake. She got up and browsed a while through the Washington Green Book. While checking the backgrounds of some of her new acquaintances she came upon Webster's name impressively indexed.

Rowena was not given to protracted brooding over any adversity. In her dressing room the magnifying hand mirror indicated no apparent deepening of the few ineradicable wrinkles. After a refreshing bath the cheval glass reassured her that while her face and figure might conceivably be less exquisite than those of a few women elsewhere, she certainly was not Number Seven in Washington.

She lay down for a half-hour's relaxation before dressing, and her customary balancing of the day's experiences. Yes, it was all in focus now. She had exasperated herself over Claudie Bracque to take her mind off Eleanor Quilling's infuriating indecisiveness. Why was the woman so damned hesitant about a divorce? She had had two husbands before Tony. Was his father's serious illness a factor? Not likely. Eleanor was still young and could marry several titles as good as Tony's would be. And Tony said she had long known his inheritance wouldn't bring him a penny more than he had already . . . . Hey! What if Papa authorized Tony to offer Eleanor a settlement? Of course, that would do it! When Papa saw how much it meant to his little girl . . . Oh, what a wonderful solution!

She pressed the telephone's pantry button. Phillips, the butler, responded.

"Yes, ma'am, the Senator's dining at home, Miss McGravey."

Right, right, right! Even if Papa was having guests, there would be plenty of time for her.

She closed her eyes in rapturous contemplation. *The Countess of Harrock. Rowena, Countess of Harrock?* No, that was when you were born to the title. Very well, *the Countess of Harrock.* And mistress of Broome Abbey. It was like being fifteen again. *The Countess of Har . . .*

The by-no-means seventh most beautiful woman in Washington was asleep.

The evening was pleasantly warm. Newton and Timmy Thackaray took their coffee cups out on the terrace of Timmy's East Side apartment. Below them the clamor of the daytime streets was quieting to a sleepy murmur. Distant neon signs across the river were blinking like fireflies.

Newton felt a curious repose as he reported details about his acquisition.

"Your dad had the realty department examine the title. I'd forgotten fifty acres could assure so much privacy."

"Will it need much repairing?"

"None structurally. The first Elkins had a lot to do with its planning, though he gave the credit to an Italian architect he'd brought over in one of his trading vessels. The beams are all black oak fourteen inches thick and pinned together like the ribs of a ship. The double floors are black oak, too, all hand planed and satin smooth. A lot of the original eighteenth-century furnishings are as usable as the day they were made. Even the toys in the nursery are ready and waiting to withstand another generation of kids."

"Now all you need is the wife to provide them."

"Yes," said Newton.

Timothy Thackaray, Senior, was puzzled as he looked across his desk at Newton's ungainly figure. It was not like Newton to be so unresponsive. An hour ago, when General Brockner at the Pentagon had enthusiastically approved his suggestion that Newton attend the meeting, Thackaray's satisfaction had been in no small part paternal. The boy's hesitance now caused the same personal concern Thackaray would have felt had Timmy been sitting there. It must be due to something more than a consideration of his work schedule.

"They'll want you in Washington only a day or two. I'll send Clarkson and Robey along in case you want graphs and figures." Newton, of course, would need little assistance. His fantastic memory could produce data as fast as the files of the Micro Division. Thackaray suppressed an impulse to add that eighty million dollars in space craft orders could ensue from Newton's appearance: at the moment such potentials might have little weight in the boy's considerations. Newton's eyes continued to be fixed absently on one of the paperweights on Thackaray's desk, a silver miniature of the Prometheus engine Newton's heat shield had helped to perfect.

"The Pentagon says your being there will insure a full committee."

Newton clenched his first. "The Pentagon must have circulated that piece in *Short*."

"What piece?" Mr. Thackaray was obviously unaware of it.

"I'm sorry," said Newton. "I assumed you had seen it."

"Newton, what the hell is this? I'm completely in the dark."

"It's an article ostensibly about the company. It came out last week and it's just about destroyed my private life. I can't go to the Y without being asked stupid questions and scribbling autographs. I'm not built for public display."

Thackaray remembered Barstow, the head of Public Relations,

mentioning that *Short* wanted to do a story on Thackaray Dynamics. It was four months ago when Barstow had been with him in Milan at the ground-breaking of the Italian plant. He recalled agreeing with Barstow that *Short's* vast circulation made the idea appealing. Reminded now of Newton's inherent shyness, Thackaray felt a twinge of self-reproach. He should have asked Barstow for details.

"Is there much about you?"

"Only a few paragraphs. But the damned thing makes me out a Wonder Man. Brief but nauseating."

Thackaray was silent. There would be no use telling Newton his modest opinion of himself was not generally shared.

"I'm sorry, Newton," said Thackaray, although there was nothing apologetic in his tone. Newton looked up. "This invitation isn't from a fan club. It's for a private consultation with a Senate study group. You'll admit you're more familiar with selenology than most people."

Newton was silent a moment, then abruptly slapped his knees as he often did when relieved from stress. His face relaxed in a rueful grin.

"Thanks. I'm hypersensitive sometimes. When do I go?"

Thackaray smiled. "The meeting's at ten Thursday morning, but General Brockner would like to brief you Wednesday night on what may come up."

After Newton had gone Thackaray asked for a copy of the *Short* interview. Barstow himself appeared with it. He wasted no time reporting that the piece had made all of *Short's* foreign editions, insuring more than thirty million readers, and sat with glowing contentment as Thackaray read it through.

It was titled "They Are Planning Tomorrow's World" and dealt with that group of alumni of the Massachusetts Institute of Physics who, because of their creative concern with mankind's needs twenty and thirty years from now, had been labeled Futurians. Many of their projects were at present in abeyance because the proper tools for realizing them did not yet exist. They ranged from novel housekeeping facilities, which in a few decades would be commonplace, to several startling advances in the field of cybernetic organisms. Of the seven Futurian inventions either already changing America's living habits or soon to be available, four had sprung from the brain of Newton Bemis, chief biophysicist of Thackaray Dynamics and acknowledged by his fellows to be the brightest star in the Futurian galaxy. While most of his present activities pertained to interplanetary biology, he was reported to be perfecting a chromergic device which would fuelize color rhythms for the preparation of food in tomorrow's kitchens.

There was a thumbnail biography. He was a native of Granton, Vermont, twenty-nine years old, and unmarried. His wiry body was curiously slender for a man six feet one in height. He had blue-gray eyes set deep in a face as long and plain as Lincoln's and, while conversing, was given to raking his fingers through his thick black hair. He played handball twice a week at New York's West Side YMCA and engaged in frequent matches at the Morgan and International Chess Clubs. The interviewer had found him brusquely dismissive of his talents and professional activities. An unnamed former classmate described him as essentially an idealist convinced that despite today's grim realities, the indomitable virtue in man's nature would eventually halt his career of self-destruction. One of his associates recalled his once saying, "I guess I'm a physicist, because by working with incontrovertible facts, I may stumble on a fragment of incontrovertible truth."

Thackaray finished reading. There was nothing in it to which anyone but Newton could have objected.

"How does it add up?" Barstow asked cagily. Sometimes Thackaray found flaws in perfection.

"It's good. Unhappily, Newton Bemis regards it as an invasion of privacy."

"My God, did he come to you about it?"

"He wouldn't have mentioned it if we hadn't been discussing something else. Did you hear from him?"

"Not directly. *Short* happened to send their most personable woman reporter to interview him. When she phoned me from the reception desk I thought she'd melt the intercom. Bemis had practically kicked her out of his office. She said she wondered if it had been because she was female."

"Surely, she didn't think Newton . . ."

"Oh, I straightened her out. When she calmed down she admitted he'd been completely masculine. But she insists he hates all women."

"He didn't at M.I.P. My son says he almost married the daughter of the Dean. He became interested in her when she invited him to join a group of students concerned with eugenic engineering."

"What might that be?"

"It had something to do with surgery to improve the human skeleton. I believe at the time there were discussions on possible improvements of the knee and ankle. In those days, Newton was ready to explore any field of knowledge."

"Maybe the girl wanted to experiment on him."

Thackaray laughed. "Newton would have answered any call for volunteers. I don't know why they broke it off. Anyway, he hates having laymen look on him as Mr. Wizard. And until he's reconciled, let's try to keep him out of print."

"O.K." Barstow concealed his frustration. *"Life* and *Paris-Match* wanted pictures of him at work."

"Too bad." Thackaray turned his attention to the correspondence on his desk. Barstow rose. Thackaray's voice followed him to the door. "And have Security give him any seclusion he might want. I wouldn't like being a character witness at a murder trial."

Chapter 2

Newton found it easy to identify the five members of the Senate study group. They had all been in the movie clips General Brockner had run off at last night's briefing. The deep surf booming of Senator Trigger, the honey-drip cadences of Senator Cokeley, the pneumatic-drill-let's-have-no-nonsense staccato of Senator Fendriss, and the plaintive, nasal whinny of Senator Bixdry were all immediately recognizable. The one who asked no questions must be Senator McGravey. He would be there, General Brockner had said, because of his knowledge of finance rather than spatial activities.

Newton was much more at ease than he had expected to be. Apparently, that idiotic piece in *Short* had not been read by the Senators. At least, no one mentioned it. And this morning his questioners sought only scientific information. It was encouraging to find them particularly interested in the potentials of remote microscopy. Senator Fendriss' angry barks on the sound track were evidently not habitual. When Newton asked if his statement on lunar oxygen had been sufficiently informative, Senator Fendriss almost cooed his "No, please tell us more."

"Like any other engine," Newton amplified, "Man's body will always need fuel. His normal machine energy depends on the conversion of about seven pounds of food a day. Even with the recycling of human waste on moon trips, he will need a daily oxygen ration in liquid form of approximately two pounds. So selenologists are concerned with the possibility of getting oxygen from lunar dust and metals."

Senator Bixdry, one of the most informed members of the Agriculture and Forestry Committee, had experienced moments of bewilderment during Newton's explanation that pions were really pi mesons and muons were mu mesons and that their X-ray decay had led to the comparatively new field of science, neutrino physics. Now he had a question. "Have you ever tasted that algae flour?"

"No, sir," Newton confessed. "I'm not familiar with their experiments, but reports on the Colorado program are available. It embraces research on all forms of friendly bacteria. They believe that in the near future a tank of green liquid can be the spaceman's wheat field."

While most of Newton's technicalities eluded him, Senator Clovis McGravey listened with mounting respect. His foresight had made him an investor in the early days of Thackaray Dynamics. He had not needed the reprint from *Short* he had found among his briefing data to inform him of Newton Bemis' value as a Thackaray asset.

At the lunch recess the Senator returned to his office where a message from Rowena had said she would be waiting. No doubt she wanted to report on Quilling's offer to his wife. Maybe the money could be paid in four installments. That would be much handier for tax purposes.

Rowena was telephoning when he arrived. "All right, dear," said Rowena, "I'll be there in fifteen minutes," and hung up.

"Tony?"

"No, Webster. He's taking me to lunch."

"Did Tony open negotiations?"

"I've been wondering. I know they're definitely closed."

"She wouldn't listen?"

"I doubt that she was asked to. Anyway, let's just say my interest in Tony Quilling is now terminated. Don't look so dejected, darling. Truly, it's no unbearable loss."

It was hard to detect how deeply Rowena had been disappointed. She had always kept her strongest feelings to herself. He had first noticed it when Rowena was fourteen and Orvie Swayne's aphrodisiac voice was catnip to the bobby sox world. He had casually asked her if she were among Swayne's admirers. He could remember her devious reply. "The girls at school think he's divine and he's chartered them to form an official Orvie Swayne club. I definitely wouldn't join such a stupid club in a million years." A few days later the McGravey housekeeper reported that Rowena's secret treasures included a score of Swayne records and a dozen photographs, one of which had been inscribed, "With sincere good wishes to Rowena MacGravey." The "MacGravey" had explained her prior suggestion that the family adopt that form of the name.

"Care to tell me what happened?"

"When Tony went home last night, Eleanor had a little surprise waiting. She's going to have a baby. This morning he was kind enough to admit he had been a bit of a fibber when he told me they hadn't lived together for six months." Rowena got up. "And thus endeth our little romance. So-o-o—" Rowena lightly bestowed a filial kiss and walked briskly to the office door—"I'm lunching with Webster."

"You don't want to tell me a little more about it?"

"No. You might feel sorry for me and I might feel sorry for me and it would all be very dreary. Anyway, I'm a little confused and want to put it out of my mind for awhile. Webster knows nothing about it and won't ask questions."

"Before you go, let me say I never thought too highly of Tony and I'm glad you're going to forget him. And while I don't mean to tell you what you should do, I've rather hoped that it might be Webster who . . ."

"Then no advice, please, Papa. Cheer up. I'll tell you when I want it. Thanks, darling, for trying to help."

She leaned back in the taxi.

"Eleanor does need me, dearest, and I know I'd feel grizzly all my life if I left her now." What touching concern for poor, devoted little Eleanor. *"But, my darling, of course I was going to ask her. And I still want you terribly. But now there's nothing we can do, is there?"* He needn't have been so smugly reconciled to his wife's condition. Anyway, to hell with him. Actually, there had been nothing there except those looks and that goddamned smile.

Webster was as sweet and uninquisitive as Rowena had expected him to be. He was stimulated by some news of his own.

"The Secretary, of course, didn't definitely promise it, but he did ask how fluent my Italian was. I didn't know anyone in Rome was resigning."

"I did," said Rowena.

"Who?"

"Wally Ingliss. He's the Second Secretary, isn't he?"

Webster was astonished. "Rowena, how on earth did you learn that?"

"His sister Marjorie told me yesterday at Edouard, the Confessor's."

Webster laughed. "Maybe the F.B.I. should screen Edouard's beauticians."

"But that would be the vacancy, wouldn't it?"

"Yes."

"You didn't know it?"

"No, I didn't. Gosh!"

Webster seldom displayed such animation. With a little encouragement, he would include her in his assignment to Rome. Being the wife of a Second Secretary would not be very glamorous, but Webster was wealthy, too, and with Papa's influence could rise to posts not usually attainable by career men. They finished their coffee.

"Would you like to talk some more about it tonight, Webster?"

"I thought you were booked."

"I might get free. Phone me before you leave."

"Right."

Having dropped Webster at State, Bates turned the car toward

Georgetown. Rowena closed her eyes and began to form a program. The only way to make a complete erasure of Tony Quilling was, of course, to marry someone else; plunge into an entirely fresh existence and feel alive and three-dimensional again. Her pocket engagement book indicated the evening was free, but if she gave it to Webster, should she be prepared to reward him for his long devotion? He had said he would be at his office until six. There was ample time to consider other eligibilities. Fortunately, several were on her list. Boko Marshall's obligatory lengthy visits to his mines in Canada and Peru promised lots of freedom, but raising two step-daughters would have to be considered. Last week, Andy Prescott had again ardently renewed his offer. Andy was certainly personable, and while it would be easy to keep him from running for Governor, nevertheless, marrying him would mean spending at least four months a year in Texas. There was Steve Preston. Steve had even more money than Papa. He was certainly no older than Janet Pryor's husband, and where could you find a happier wife than Janet? Another point in Steve's favor was his having so many lovely houses in so many countries. There were those two dwellings facing Gracie Square, neither of which he had ever occupied. Last month he had been undecided whether to sell or raze them and put up a modern house. If she married him, the decision would rest with her. It might be rather wonderful to commission Ormond Fannestock to design one for her. No one had built an impressive mansion in New York for years and Ruthie Wayne was insufferably smug about that tropical villa Fannestock had designed for her in Antigua. The idea of calling a thirty-room palace a "fun cottage"! No, Steve must not be lightly dismissed. What a pity Alec Tengler was no longer available. She had been a fool to drop him when Tony came along. Alec was wonderfully important at Cape Kennedy now, telling all those astronauts what to do. The girl he had married was a very dull creature, but that was little comfort.

Newton had planned to dine alone and not to be interrupted in enjoying the excitements of the latest Brookhaven Report. He had been able only to nibble at it once or twice since boarding the plane in New York. How much could that gradient synchrotrone at Brookhaven reveal of the infinite system within the hydrogen atom? What a striking reversal of the traditional relationship of human beings to the universe. Above the firmament of the atom, man was now himself a vast infinity instead of a mote in the eye of the theologian's God. It would be a nice gambit to offer Timmy in their next Why session.

When the study group adjourned for the day, Senator McGravey altered his own schedule. Newton, anticipating interrogation which might increase the Senator's understanding of space problems, accepted his invitation to dinner.

"What time, sir?"

"Oh, about seven," said the Senator. "It's only ten minutes from your hotel to Georgetown."

At five Rowena had thoroughly indexed all her matrimonial possibilities and decided to have dinner with Webster, and was again toying with the idea of going with him to Rome as a bride. Her telephone rang.

"Rowena?"

"Yes, Papa."

"Does the name Newton Bemis mean anything to you?"

"No. Why?"

"He's dining with me at seven. I'd like you to meet him. If you're going out you'll have time to say hello. Go down to the study. In the brief case on my desk you'll see a magazine clipping. It will tell you something about him. How do you feel?"

"Much better, Papa."

"Good. G'bye, dear."

"I'd like you to meet him" usually nominated her to be hostess to one of Papa's important constituents. Most were bores whose attentions were either exhaustingly polite or clumsily romantic. Rowena went downstairs dutifully to inform herself on Mr. Bemis.

Phillips, in the study doorway, had to say "Excuse me, Miss Mc-Gravey" twice before Rowena looked up from her reading. "It's Mr. Harris on the phone, Ma'am. I didn't know if you were in or not."

Rowena meditated. "I'll call him back in a few minutes."

When she did, his secretary reported that Webster's line was busy.

"I don't think he'd mind my cutting in, Miss McGravey."

"No, don't disturb him. Just tell him, please, that I'm afraid I won't be free this evening and will talk with him tomorrow. Thank you."

Among the briefing data on the Senator's desk was an extract from an article in *The Saturday Review*. A secretarial note said it was a comment on Sir Bernard Lovell's book, *The Exploration of Outer Space*. The review had been written by Ralph E. Lapp. It mentioned the early experiments by Carl Jansky and Grote Rebers in mapping the radio sky and the eventual achievement by England's Jodrell Bank radio telescope in recording the impact on the moon of the first Soviet Lunik rocket. After reading it, Rowena telephoned Myron Cobb at the Naval Observatory. Her talk with him was brief but informative.

As she entered the library, Papa was breaking the conversational ice with his Why-I-gave-up-gin pick.

"The gin sold in England is seventy proof, which is why the martinis there are as good as you can find anywhere. But the gin they send us is never less than eighty-five or ninety proof. They haven't learned that Americans who want firewater can get it in other forms. I think that's the main reason we're drinking so much eighty proof vodka these days. Ah, here's my child, Mr. Bemis."

Two years ago, Webster Harris had seen Rowena from a distance and had had time to regain his poise before they first met. Tonight Newton was denied even a moment for adjustment. Happily the dazzling creature before him was equipped with conversational oxygen. She smiled encouragingly as she administered it.

"Are you in politics, Mr. Bemis?"

Looking at her sharply, the Senator explained Mr. Bemis was a scientist down from New York for consultation. Rowena's expression of pleasure on learning that Newton was a physicist and her unaffected eagerness to hear anything he might care to say gave Newton time to regain his composure.

"Are you staying at a hotel?"

Newton tried to be amusing about the switchboard gadgets at the top of his hotel bed: one button reflected on the ceiling the hands of a clock, another caused vocal announcements of the outside temperature and barometric pressure, a whole series regulated a color television set across the room. The Senator chuckled. His startlingly lovely daughter smiled appreciatively.

Rowena was coordinating her jumbling thoughts: *Perhaps the most promising biophysicist in the world.* How could one possibly fuelize color rhythms? Not yet thirty, yet the Pentagon considers his advice as important as Von Braun's. She recalled Alec Tengler's uncertainty about what might follow the NASA program. Was the Prometheus engine, which *Short* said Bemis had perfected, even more important than the reorganized Nova? His face was more boyish than the pictures in *Short* indicated. It was pleasant to sense his consciousness of herself. Or was it instinctive shyness that made him hesitant to share the relaxed mood she and Papa were inviting? He reminded her of someone tantalizingly familiar and elusive. Who? It was like groping for a raspberry seed with your tongue. That long nose, the wide mouth and the lanky frame of his body provided no assistance.

"How long will you be with us, my boy?"

"I'm not certain, sir. I'll go back to New York tomorrow if the Committee is finished with me then."

The raspberry seed dislodged itself. It wasn't his appearance, but his voice. It had the exciting voltage of Orvie Swayne, the lightly erotic stimulus that had stirred a fourteen year-old schoolgirl. But this was no jukebox hypnotist. She had at her disposal a new and highly eligible admirer, a genius, with a fantastically brilliant career ahead of him.

Chapter 3

Newton murmured, "No, thank you," and the hostess with her armful of magazines moved to the rear of the plane. With the Brookhaven report unopened on his lap he deliberated the surprising development of his Washington visit.

Last night by accident he had met a girl luminous with charm and beauty. So it was not a natural law that all good-looking women were inwardly deficient. The few he knew were so insecure they constantly baited their conversation for reassuring compliments. Miss McGravey's was ego-free, engaging and intelligent. Her small-talk sparkled with humor rather than vapid flippancies. Her serious opinions were uttered modestly. Nine women out of ten with conversational talent threw their convictions at you like bricks. Miss McGravey's gentle womanliness required no verbal victories to satisfy its needs. Her mature mentality silently invited alterations to possibly unsound beliefs. How rarely you found that kind these days.

How old was she? Perhaps twenty-four, though her skin and complexion had a teen-age youngness. Why wasn't she married? She was unquestionably built for it. No man could fail to recognize in the structure of her pelvic area the haunch bones of a born mother. Maybe she didn't yet want children. Maybe she was happily in love and quite satisfied with a relationship that didn't include marriage. Was it his own increasing maturity that enabled him to think of her so objectively? Even so, he realized he had been greatly stirred by her presence. He still heard the low music of her laughter, especially during dinner. It had a soothing, slumbrous quality as soft as the candle glow on the tray of flowers within their Georgian silver fence in the center of the table. It was laughter that might add greatly to the serenity of an eighteenth-century house.

If she had a lover, he must be away somewhere, as she could dine with Newton almost any night next week. Had she accepted his invitation out of compassion? Or did she really want to play with him on that handsome chessboard in the library? She probably was a good player. Anyway, despite the awkwardness he had undoubtedly exhibited, she had not graded him as a complete clown.

"I think I've seen pictures of her," said Timmy, "but I hadn't guessed she was such a knockout. How did it happen?"

"After yesterday's session her father asked me to dinner, thinking we'd be alone. He wanted some information on costs I hadn't gone into. At the last minute her dinner date was canceled so she joined us."

"And she's got a good brain?"

"Oh, yes. She got a B.A. in sociology at Bennington. She'd planned to have a couple of years at the Sorbonne, but when her father got elected she came with him to Washington to run his household. Another thing I like is her intellectual modesty. The space program is almost a mystery to her father. During dinner Rowena laughed when he confessed that until the subject had come up at the afternoon session, he had believed interplanetary pod stations were related to spatial plant growth. He wasn't really annoyed, but her laughter made him say: 'All right, do *you* know what they are?'

"He seemed as surprised as I was when she quoted Ralph Lapp, Alec Tengler and half a dozen other people." Now Timmy sensed as much awe as ardor in Newton's recounting. "You wouldn't expect her knowledge to include the operation of the Jodrell Bank radiotelescope. She asked if I knew anything about Sir Bernard Lovell's recent progress with it. Then she almost bowled me over by asking if the thirty-foot 'dish' put up by Grote Rebers in his back yard in Wheaton, Illinois, wasn't perhaps the first important experiment in radio astronomy."

"When are you going to see her again?"

"Thursday. If I can catch an early afternoon plane, she's going to show me the Japanese cherry blossoms before dinner. If I don't fly back too late, I'll phone you."

"She really hit you, didn't she?"

"I know I want to see her again."

After his third visit to Georgetown, Newton pictured evenings of felicity across the chessboard in Rowena's company. Years of playing with her father had given her an empiric grasp of chess fundamentals. Newton rated her game somewhere between that of Timmy, who still trusted Ponziani's opening despite a hundred disastrous developments, and that of the better-than-average Dr. Ruke, Newton's favorite opponent among chess club regulars. Newton learned that neither Rowena nor her father had ever deliberately employed a P-Q4 opening for White. Rowena was grateful to learn its advantages. And while she had never known their technical names, her use both of Philador's and Petroff's defenses evidenced easy familiarity. She was thoughtful and adroit and could become excellent under the guidance of a proficient teacher. It was warmly rewarding to find her so eager to learn.

The night of his latest visit to Washington, Rowena's obligation as a patroness had taken them to an orchestral concert. During the intermission Rowena questioned Newton about a match he had attended the night before in New York. He recounted some brilliant hypermodern replies to a seeming impregnable Alekhine defense. Ten minutes later they were being demonstrated in the library on N Street, the promise of Moussorgsky's "Pictures at an Exhibition," which Newton liked enormously, completely forgotten.

Less than a month after Rowena entered his life, Newton asked her to share the rest of it. It occurred a few days after Rowena had agreed that her inspection of his Vermont house might help resolve some of his uncertainties about its refurbishing.

"If we drove up next Saturday, Newton, we could spend the night with Nina and Dick Farrell in Bennington. Nina was in my class and Dick teaches there now. Their house can't be more than twenty miles from you, so you ought to meet them. On Sunday morning I could see your place and then you could take me back to New York in the evening. How does that sound?"

"Wonderful!" Newton tried to say normally.

"But you sort of promised to keep this weekend free, honey," Senator McGravey reminded his daughter. "I told the Judge and his wife you'd fly out with me."

Rowena took her father's hand. "Papa, would you want me to be wasting time at somebody's silver wedding when I ought to be giving serious consideration to my first?"

The Senator was startled. He had noted with pleasure the increased frequency of Newton's visits, but, he had reminded himself, with the Tony Quilling experience, Rowena had seen four romances—perhaps more?—die in the bud. No matter how eligible her present suitor, now that she was thirty it was unlikely that she would allow her heart to run away with her head again. Newton, he had assumed, was in the early stages of a careful screening process.

"Newton's asked you to marry him?"

"Not yet. But I shouldn't be surprised if he did this weekend. I've finally met the man I want, Papa. Thank you for finding him.

I must dash." A gentle pat on his cheek emphasized her gratitude. The Senator watched her go in silent awe. Down his cheeks came tears generated by equal parts of love and relief.

Rowena's talent for organization manifested itself on the Vermont weekend. Newton had revealed an almost virginal shyness during his courtship. He had kissed her only once, hesitantly, a kiss imbued more with respect than passion. If effective action were not taken, Rowena recognized, she would have acquired merely a more attractive equerry than Webster.

Careful deliberation resulted in the selection of the Farrells as overnight hosts. Good weather would facilitate operations, but rain would not be a handicap—in fact it might even serve as a stimulus.

From the moment he was welcomed, Newton responded to the serenity of the Farrell household. It glowed with marital happiness. At cocktail time it was cool enough to warrant a fire in the living room. With the Farrell's endearing two-year-old daughter cuddled on his lap, Newton gave up trying to rationalize his feelings; the beautiful creature across the room, smiling so tenderly at his rapport with small Miranda, could bring stability and order into his life.

When Newton returned to New York, Timmy had gone to the company's Seattle plant for staff conferences. Newton telephoned him and asked if Timmy would be his best man.

"Of course I will," beamed Timmy. "At your rate of progress I suppose I'd better fly back tomorrow."

Newton laughed. "Tomorrow Rowena's going to find out when the cathedral in Washington will be available. We'll be married there, probably in October."

"Hot damn! You and I in striped pants and cutaway coats, I presume."

"If you prefer we can just hunt up a justice of the peace."

"No, let's humor the bride. Some day I may marry the same church-minded type and we'll both need them again."

"I didn't learn much, Dad," said Timmy thoughtfully. "I'm sure of one thing; she's more beautiful than her photographs indicate."

"What's under the beauty?"

"A quick mind. And she laughs easily. Meeting her fiancé's closest friend might make any bride-to-be self-conscious, and possibly that affected the atmosphere last night. At dinner there was more chatter than conversation. After the theater we went to the Plaza for a nightcap and there she let Newt and me do most of the talking. At first I thought perhaps she was tired, but before long I had the feeling I was under a microscope. Of course, I might have been wrong."

"Perhaps you made her feel she was, too."

"If I did, she certainly concealed it."

Father and son were silent as the waiter removed their lunch plates.

"Well, if Newton's in such a state of bliss, it could be he's found exactly the right girl."

"Let's hope so. But you can't rely on his judgment of women."

"I'd hardly call Newton a child."

"I would about matrimony. Maybe that's nature balancing his gifts in other areas. As a lover, he could be blind as a bat. I'm sure he thinks he loves Rowena. He also thought he loved Betsy. Even today, he doesn't realize that for Betsy he had more admiration than love. Thank God, Betsy had enough sense to face facts and call it off. What scares me is that if now he's been caught in a trap, it'd be too late should he try to fight his way out."

Mrs. Blanche Colton Beehouse's social management schedule for October was crowded with debutante parties, but when the cathedral's dean was persuaded to change Rowena's wedding day from the sixth of October to the twelfth, Mrs. Beehouse consented to take it on. This pleased Rowena greatly, as the prestige of Mrs. Beehouse would insure the proper journalistic attention both in America and abroad. Her office, she promised Rowena, would immediately alert *The Diplomat, Vogue, Harper's Bazaar,* the good English picture weeklies and important journals in other countries, so that proper space would be reserved for photographs and copy. Rowena's uncertainty about the attitude of *Le Monde du Chic* was quickly dispelled. Mrs. Beehouse revealed Paul Bracque was an old friend. She made Rowena even happier with her confidential news that the publisher and his wife had recently separated.

"I like them all," said Newton truthfully.

"Thank you, darling. I think this one will be best for newspapers. The light contrasts are sharper."

Rowena replaced in their bulky envelope the proofs of the photographs taken for the engagement announcements, and told the Passy hat-check girl to put them with her other packages. She and Newton left the lounge and went in to their table.

It had been an exhausting day for Rowena. She had arrived in New York at ten. Consideration of the preliminary sketches for her bridal dress had taken up most of the forenoon. Then there had been her lunch with Janet Pryor. Janet had been one of Rowena's earliest admirers at boarding school and, as editor of the junior yearbook, had captioned Rowena's photograph "She walks in beauty like the night." Janet's election as president of the senior class had been largely due to Rowena's vigorous campaigning. As a member of the nominating committee, Rowena had opposed the selection of Harriet Fanning, one of the prettiest and most popular girls in the class, but in whom Rowena's keen insight had detected envy, a trait she could not condone. "Let us remember, this is not a beauty contest," Rowena had pointed out firmly, "and we're not electing a Miss Ogden Academy. Attractive profiles are hardly the basic qualifications for class presidents. So I nominate Janet Pryor. She has intelligence, a noble character, and a fine academic record, qualities far beyond mere prettiness. And we all know her sweet, generous nature."

As a reward for Janet's idolatry through the years, Rowena invited her to be her matron of honor. Janet gratefully accepted the invitation and assured Rowena she would be the most beautiful bride ever seen.

The rest of the afternoon had been taken up by conferences with Mrs. Beehouse and other important activities, so that she had been unable to see Newton until they met at the restaurant for dinner. Newton was surprised to learn of the mountain of responsibilities a fiancée must shoulder. Admiring Rowena's cheerful acceptance of them he felt a bit guilty. "I wish I could take some of them off your hands."

"They're a bride's job, my sweet," said Rowena, buoyantly.

When the headwaiter left with their order, Rowena produced a little list of items requiring discussion. Newton confessed that other than asking Timmy to be his best man, he had as yet selected no other groomsmen. He willingly agreed to include Rowena's oldest and dearest Washington friend, Webster Harris, among his ushers.

"Papa's taken the Chevy Chase for the engagement dance. We discovered neither the Sulgrave nor the F Street Club would be large enough. Oh, dear, what is this next item? I wrote it in a taxi." Newton tried to help.

"It looks like a capital *N* with a small *v* and *t*," he ventured. "Or could it be a *w* and *t*?"

"Yes. It's a *w*. Your white tie. Do you have formal evening clothes, dear?"

"Just a dinner jacket."

"You'll need tails." Rowena regarded his appearance. "Go to a very good tailor, and tell him you'll need it a week from Thursday."

"But the Chevy Chase party isn't until the thirtieth."

"Yes, my darling. But on the eighteenth we're going to a dinner

‡ 34 ‡

at the British Embassy. There'll be a lot of dear friends I'll want you to meet."

Newton dutifully jotted the date in his notebook. He was elated to know that Rowena wanted to show him to her friends. It was also warming to recognize another promise of their life together. Rowena would happily take on the burden of handling their social responsibilities.

Rowena was again checking the list. "Why are you smiling?" Newton asked.

"Because I have a lovely surprise for you. Look at this. What does it say?"

" 'House.' "

"Yes, my love. Papa's going to see that we have one." Rowena's smile was that of a happy child. Newton felt a bit dense.

"But we have a house, darling. One we both love."

"Of course, sweet, but we won't be staying in Vermont the whole year. Didn't you say we'd live in New York for months at a time?"

"I did indeed. And that's why I renewed the lease on the flat. I thought you liked it very much."

"Oh, I do. And that's where we'll be staying for a year at least." Rowena laughed. "Forgive me, darling. I adore your am-I-going-to-like-oysters look. How would you like to own a Fannestock house?"

"I've never thought about such a thing."

"I have and so has Papa. I told him it would be absolute heaven to have a kitchen designed for your color cones and a study you wouldn't have to leave when you wanted to read reference material in microfilm libraries."

Newton chuckled. "With the work I have piled up, I wouldn't be able to complete that telereader for at least two years."

"But you've nothing against having a house in New York, have you?"

"I suppose not. But—"

"Then that's what we'll have. Papa's bought two of those old

‡ 35 ‡

residences on East End Avenue near Gracie Square. As soon as you and I decide what we want, down they'll come and up will go ours. Do you know Ormond Fannestock?"

"By reputation."

"Papa and I talked with him yesterday. He knows all about you and says he could think of nothing more wonderful than creating a Futurian house, at least one that can accommodate your inventions as they come along. He's going to Ceylon next week for the opening of his university buildings there, but before he leaves, he'll meet you any time to discuss his ideas."

It was painful to have to check Rowena's enthusiasm. Newton took one of her trembling hands. "My darling, have you any idea what such a house would cost?"

"No, and does it actually matter?"

"I'm afraid it does. It might cost a million dollars."

Rowena pressed his hand to her heart. "My very youngest child, the father of the girl you are going to marry happens to be very rich. He also happens to love us both. He would be happy to make it a wedding present. Why do you look so wounded?"

"I couldn't possibly accept such a gift."

Rowena laughed. "Then you don't have to, my dear."

"I don't?"

"No. Because Daddy said he expected you might feel that way, so whatever is needed for the house can be a loan, and I can promise Daddy won't worry about how much he lends us, or when, if ever, we paid him back."

Newton made an effort at lightness. "Mother, dear, someday when I am rich, I'll build you any kind of house you want. Right now, I can't. And I can't possibly let your father lend me money."

Rowena released his hand. "Why not?"

"Because I have what a psychiatrist might call a nursery fixation. I don't wonder at your staring, but it's true. I don't expect ever to shake it off, and, now that I mention it, I don't believe I'll ever try to. I think I told you that I'd wanted to own the Elkins house even when I was a boy."

"And that your father was too poor to buy it. But darling, what can that possibly have to do—"

"I didn't tell you something else about my father." Newton's voice was below its usual conversational level. "When I was ten, my father's partner in a lumber company embezzled most of the firm's capital. I had no notion of how hard we'd been hit. My mother had just died, and I assumed that the subsequent change in our living habits—we had to give up our old house and take rooms in the village—had something to do with father's grief.

"Somewhere I heard that Mr. and Mrs. Elkins were going to California. I didn't know it was just for a visit, and assumed their house would be vacated. This was exciting news to me, because a stream that ran through the Elkins' property led to a wonderful natural swimming pool. For years in the summertime, Granton kids had monopolized it. After young Tommy Elkins almost drowned in it, Mrs. Elkins told us we couldn't use it anymore. When I heard she and her husband were going away, I hurried to my father and told him we could have a house of our own again. I pointed out that I was a very good swimmer and would be safe in the Elkins pond and that the stove in the big Elkins kitchen produced the most wonderful doughnuts in the world. My father said, 'Come here, Newty.' When I went to his side, he hugged me and said he, too, would like to have the Elkins place, but it wasn't for sale. 'So let's just forget all about it, shall we?' I said, 'Yes, sir,' and tried to.

"I was quickly reconciled to living in the boarding house because a hero of mine, catcher on the Granton High School baseball team, lived there, too. He was sixteen and quite grown up to me. Occasionally he let me talk with him. When I told him of my father's regret that the Elkins place was not for sale, he laughed. 'That's a good one,' he said. 'What would he have bought it with? Hot air?' I didn't know what he meant and hazarded that money would more likely have been used. He laughed again and walked away.

"The truth was that I hadn't the dimmest knowledge of my

father's finances until one day when Mr. Sharples, who owned the general store, asked me if I'd like to deliver groceries for him on Saturdays. He added something to the effect it might please my father to see me trying to increase the family income. For the first time it dawned on me that we might be poor. That evening I asked my father if what I could earn would help him. He smiled and said, 'Why, I don't need anything, Newty. But thanks very much for offering to help me. If you want to work for Mr. Sharples, go ahead, but the money you make will belong to you.' 'What'll I do with it?' I asked. My father said, 'You need money for ice-cream sodas and other necessities. I suggest that anything you don't have to spend, you save. Then ten or twenty years from now if I need it, I'll come and borrow from you.' A few weeks later when I'd saved almost two dollars he praised my thrift and told me in words I could understand what solvency meant and about the pain and distress of the man who owed more than he could pay. By then I'd heard something about his business troubles and sensed that the pain and distress he spoke of were his own. He must have seen that I was sharing his anguish because he made a great effort to convince me that he wasn't worried about anything.

"Somehow he got back in business again. When I finished high school I wanted to go to work but he wouldn't allow it. I'd had pretty high marks and he insisted that putting me through college would be no strain on him. I didn't learn until my junior year at M.I.P. that almost every cent he made had gone into my education. He'd even had to sell what was left of his business. By then I knew how important it was to get a degree. Two scholarships I'd won and a part-time job took me through my senior year. The day after I graduated my father went back to Granton and I stayed on to talk with Timmy's father about working for Thackaray Dynamics. The next afternoon my father died. Our old landlady was with him. She said his heart just gave out, and that the last thing he said was 'Newty graduated *summa cum laude.*' "

Newton lifted his cocktail glass but did not bring it to his mouth.

"That may be why I get psychic ulcers when I owe more than I can pay."

Rowena checked an impulse to suggest that psychiatry might help him overcome his fixation; she could propose it later. Newton was grateful for her tender, half-whispered, "Oh, darling!"

Chapter 4

Newton's dinner at the Passy had been on Wednesday. Rowena had returned to Washington that night. Friday, Newton was lunching in the Thackaray executives' restaurant when he was summoned to the telephone.

"Sorry to interrupt your lunch, Newton." It was Mr. Thackaray's voice. "Did you say you were going to Washington for the weekend?"

"Yes, sir. On the six o'clock plane."

"Could you take the four o'clock?"

"It's ten after two. If I left within fifteen minutes. My bag's downstairs. Why?"

"I've just had a request from the State Department. They'd like to borrow you to do something for the Suruki Ambassador. That's all they cared to say over the phone. I'm to let them know if you can make it, so they can insure you a seat on the plane. They'll meet it and fill you in before they take you to the embassy."

"Do we have any dealings with Suruk? The company, I mean."

"No. Suruk is believed to have deposits of pyrochlor and euxenite. We wanted to buy some and asked ASOCO if their geologists would investigate, but they were denied entry to the interior."

"What's ASOCO?"

"Anglo-Suruki Oil Company. Actually its half American-owned."

"Could Suruk want to make its own columbium?"

"Possibly. But I don't know. Better hang up and catch that plane."

Newton finished his coffee thoughtfully. Columbium was only one of the acid resistants necessary to space vehicles. What else might Suruk produce? Tantalum? A few years ago struverite, so necessary for tantalum's preparation, had been found in the Near East, thus easing the world's dependence on Malaya for its supply. Was Suruk part of the new source? And if so, why was his advice wanted? Competent metallurgists could be found anywhere.

On the plane he searched the news columns in the evening papers for possible clues to the State Department's request. One of the weeklies provided a reference to Suruk. A correspondent in Lebanon cited the large number of luxury apartment buildings going up in Beirut. Most were business investments by wealthy *sheikhs* of oil-rich nations. One structure nearing completion was reported to have been bought by one of the many sons of the King of Suruk. Further search through the newsprint was unproductive.

The word *Suruk,* however, had a faintly familiar ring. Newton searched for it in the attic of his memory. Had he heard the word in a schoolroom? Recalling physical backgrounds sometimes brought dusty memoranda within reach.

Lilacs. From the shadowy past the scent of lilacs was demanding recognition. Lilacs he could almost see flowering somewhere in his boyhood. He was being forbidden to breathe in their delicious fragrance. Someone in Granton was talking. "*Come away from the window, Newton.*" Abruptly and vividly the lilac bush took shape. It was in full bloom outside an open window through which an eleven-year-old Newton was ecstatically inhaling its hypnotic redolence. "*We can enjoy today's wonders of nature when we finish with God's earlier experiments.*" It was Mr. Wingate speaking. Old Mr. Wingate, sympathetically shepherding a young mind slightly drugged by June back to a Sunday-school lesson. Newton returned to reality and interested himself in what Mr. Wingate was saying. He was telling the class about the Garden of Eden. He said no one was able to say exactly where Eden used to be because after the Flood subsided, Eden's rivers, the ones named in Genesis, no longer existed. The Euphrates and Tigris in the geography book had just been named after the ones in Eden. Some people said the place where Eden had been was now called Suruk. Mr. Wingate said that a mountain range that rose from Suruk's northern plains might well be the Mountain of God, which both the Bible and the Koran, a book the people in Suruk believed in, said had been the northern boundary of Eden.

Newton remembered subsequently enjoying a brief, feverish interest in Near Eastern geography and discovering that Suruk was a country on the Arabian peninsula. Measuring it with a foot ruler showed that Suruk was not quite as big as Vermont but looked like it if you turned it sideways. Either Ezekiel or Isaiah (now Newton couldn't remember which) had listed several gems abounding in Eden. He could recall nine; the sardius, the topaz, the diamond, the beryl, the onyx, the jasper, the sapphire, the emerald, and the carbuncle. The sardius had been hard to identify. Mr. Wingate had looked it up for him and said it was red, probably a kind of carnelian, and that it was worn on the high priest's breastplate. Mr. Wingate had agreed that all the jewels might have come from the Mountain of God and might still be found there if you went digging for them. Gentle Mr. Wingate. He was dead now. And so was his world of simple faith. Mr. Wingate had been spared the knowledge that miners today might be extracting from Adam's mountain what could obliterate all his descendants.

Webster Harris explained that he had asked to be assigned to meet Newton because they knew each other. As they waited for Newton's luggage, Webster confessed the State Department's paucity of information.

"We know a few things, of course. A year ago when his income was piling to a staggering figure, King Sajjid expressed willingness to let Suruk emerge from its medieval darkness. He allowed ASOCO to prepare a development plan and recommend that it be realized with UNESCO's help. Unfortunately, Sajjid attempted to begin the program without foreign guidance. Six months ago it was abruptly halted and Suruk went back to sleep again. Harvey Priest—he is one of our best Middle East experts—says the Secretary inferred from a talk with Dr. Hunain, the Suruki Ambassador, that Sajjid wants your advice about something. Dr. Hunain couldn't, or wouldn't, disclose what it was, and the Secretary didn't press him for details. The King allows Westerners to take his oil, but is reluctant to have information leave the country. Priest says he, himself, drew a blank trying to learn something by telephone from Thornton Briscoe in Suruk."

"Our ambassador?"

"Yes."

"Briscoe told him he'd had no inquiry about you from the palace, but that he would investigate. He called back ten minutes later. Nobody in the Leper Colony knew why you were wanted."

"The *Leper Colony?*"

"That's the diplomatic quarter. Do you know anything about Qam?"

"Only that it's the capital. You pronounced it as if it began with a hard *G.*"

"My feeble attempt to say it correctly. The Arabic *q* often sounds like a compromise between a throaty *g* and a *k.* For diplomats, Qam is really two communities, the old city where the King lives and the legation compound six miles to the east. The compound is a large park, reputedly the most beautiful residential district in the world. There is a highway connecting it with the city proper and Marbhein, Suruk's ancient port on the Persian Gulf, but it is without roads to other parts of the kingdom. An old palace in the Leper Colony has a throne room in which heads of missions present their letters of credence. Once or twice the King has entertained the foreigners there and paid courtesy calls at the embassies.

But most of the time he's out of reach. The only foreigner who knows him intimately is an elderly Englishman. His name is Wexford Drench, but in the compound he is known as Eustace. That's an approximation of *ustaz* which is Arabic for professor. Actually, he's a botanist. He and his wife came to Suruk when Sajjid's father was king, and they used to live in the Qam palace. Since Drench's wife died a few years ago he comes to Qam only when he wants to report to Sajjid on his experiments in the field of plant genetics. The British Ambassador says he occasionally drops in at the embassy to refresh his English speech. Now and then he brings a bit of news about the King, but not much. After Priest's first call, Briscoe telephoned the palace with the hope that Drench might be there and able to give him information. An aide told Briscoe's interpreter that Drench was there but was with His Majesty and couldn't be disturbed. I suppose Briscoe is still waiting to hear from him. Have you any conjectures?"

"Do you know if struverite has been found in Suruk?"

"Is it a mineral?"

"Yes."

"I'll ask the oil company, but I doubt that ASOCO knows much of what's happening behind the oil fields on the coast. There is even greater restraint on the movement of foreigners in Suruk than in Saudi Arabia or the Yemen. The leases entail a rigid policing of boundaries. ASOCO shares the upkeep of a couple of thousand Suruki border guards."

"What's the King afraid of?"

"We're not certain. Last year he started to use his new wealth to improve Suruki living standards. According to Drench, except for modern horticultural research, the Suruki ways of life are what they were a thousand years ago. There's a distinction, however, between Suruk and other backward nations. The death rate is lower than that of any primitive people in the world because the food they eat is excellent and plentiful. When the King decided to give his people the benefit of modern culture he had ASOCO construct an airport just outside Qam. Six months ago the develop-

ment program was halted without notice. The airport's maintenance staff was ordered back to Batrul Mina, ASOCO's main oil
port. Since then the airfield's been unused. On his recent visits to
the legation quarter, Drench has talked vaguely about a resumption of the improvement program, but except for the functioning
of the palace telephone which gets its power from Marbhein,
Suruk seems to have returned to the Middle Ages. There's another
odd thing: when we opened our embassy last year, the King
allowed Mrs. Briscoe to take photographs of him, but about the
time the development program was halted, she had to hand over
all the prints to Drench and assure him that the negatives had
been destroyed. Drench offered no reason except to say that it was
the King's wish. In the same breath came avowals from Drench of
the King's high regard for both Briscoes, so it was a bit puzzling."

"Are they still in the dark?"

"Yes. There's been some speculation on a possible connection
between the pre-emption of the photographs and the death about
the same time of one of the King's sons, a boy of fourteen. Uncon-
firmed rumors said he had been killed in the collapse of an unsound building. Expressions of grief by Arabians take many forms.

"As anything can affect the delicate relations between absolute
monarchs and oil companies, the Department was, of course, concerned. I recall that Harvey Priest was briefing us on what little
he knew about the situation when the Suruki Ambassador asked for
a meeting with the Secretary. He said his King had felt foreigners
might be disturbed by 'the recent developments' in Suruk and
wished to reassure the United States that they would in no way
affect his country's agreement with ASOCO. There was no cause
for the oil operations to be interrupted. The Ambassador added
that Suruk's withdrawal from outside contacts would continue
during a period of mourning occasioned by a death in the royal
family. The Secretary inferred the death was that of the boy in the
rumors. As the Ambassador was obviously reluctant to give details,
he was not pressed. For half a year now Dr. Hunain has continued
to express Sajjid's good will. Briscoe feels reasonably certain that

there is no sinister Russian influence at work, so the Department's official attitude is that if the King wants to seclude himself, it's none of our business."

Webster stopped his car in front of a small but impressive ultra-modern building on Massachusetts Avenue. From a silver flag staff two floors above its doorway fluttered Suruk's national banner, eleven green stripes radiating from a golden crescent in the center.

"This is the new embassy. It's been opened only a few months. They didn't have any diplomatic representatives here until the oil money started piling up less than two years ago. Then they bought a two-story frame house on E Street near George Washington University, which one of the fraternities was glad to get rid of."

The gentle brown eyes of Dr. Hunain ibn Ma'mun brightened with relief and pleasure as he shook Newton's hand. Webster, after a few obligatory politenesses, suggested that he would be happy to wait elsewhere while His Excellency and Mr. Bemis talked.

"Oh, please stay with us," urged the Ambassador, as he beckoned to a servant. "And may I offer you refreshment? Cocktails, perhaps?"

Webster and Newton were told nothing was easier to provide than vodka gimlets and the servant left the room. There were more politenesses. Dr. Hunain assured Webster that Mrs. Hunain had completely recovered from the severe cold that had deprived Washington society of her presence at various functions for more than a week. The cocktails arrived. So did tea trays spangled with hors d'oeuvres.

"Please forgive me if I do not join you," apologized Dr. Hunain "It is our month of *Ramadan* and I must take no food or drink until after dark. Are the cocktails to your liking?"

His guests pronounced them delicious and the Ambassador beamed.

"Our servants are becoming reasonably competent at mixing alcoholic drinks. It was a challenge, as the Koran forbids any judgments by taste. And now, gentlemen, to the business at hand.

"Mr. Bemis, I have the honor of inviting you to visit Suruk as His Majesty's guest. I hope that the invitation is acceptable. If so, might we discuss the date of your arrival and the length of time His Majesty may hope to entertain you?"

He leaned back in his chair and tapping his fingers looked inquiringly first at Newton and then at Webster.

Newton experienced annoyance. The Ambassador assumed a lot and had offered not a ray of enlightenment. Was His Majesty's guest expected to arrive in Suruk blindfolded?

Webster picked up the ball. "Your Excellency, Mr. Bemis will have to speak for himself."

Newton did. "I'd like to know why His Majesty wants me."

Dr. Hunain was undisturbed by Newton's bluntness. "Mr. Bemis," he said, "I shall tell you everything I know about your invitation." From his desk he picked up two officially stamped papers. "All my knowledge is from these messages. The first was received early this morning. It reads: 'His Majesty would be greatly pleased if Mr. Newton Bemis of the company called Thackaray Dynamics could come here in the very near future for consultation, the length of his stay as His Majesty's guest to be determined by Mr. Bemis.'" Dr. Hunain handed the message to Newton, and continued.

"When I learned that you were generously considering the invitation, at three o'clock this afternoon I requested further instructions." He indicated the second paper. "This is a statement telephoned a half hour later: 'His Majesty is greatly pleased to learn Mr. Bemis might visit him. Assure Mr. Bemis that acknowledgment of His Majesty's gratitude will be expressed materially as well as by hospitality.'" The second message was also passed for Newton's inspection. Dr. Hunain's discomfiture was evident as he continued.

"Mr. Bemis, I truly regret that is all I am able to tell you. I asked for more information but my superiors have not yet supplied it."

A polite cough turned Dr. Hunain to an attaché who had quietly entered the room. The man placed a third message in the Ambassador's outstretched hand.

Dr. Hunain's expression revealed nothing as he quickly read the text. He passed it to Newton. It read: "His Majesty directs me to say that no matter how brief the time Mr. Bemis elects to stay in Suruk he hopes Mr. Bemis will accept an honorarium of one million American dollars. Drench."

"The signature is that of an old friend of His Majesty who sometimes speaks for him."

At ten minutes after eight Newton and Rowena were in the library on N Street waiting for the Senator's car to take them to dinner.

"Dr. Hunain seemed as puzzled as Webster and I," recounted Newton. "He assured me no struverite had been found in Suruk. He's also certain there's no interest there in making columbium and if there's to be any development of Suruk's euxenite deposits, he hadn't heard of it. Webster signaled me to stop pressing for answers so I gave up. After we left Webster said he believed Dr. Hunain had been telling us all he knew and that our guesses would be as good as his. I said I was tired of guessing and Webster told me not to worry. The Department will send my regrets."

Phillips announced that the car had arrived. Rowena uncurled her legs from under her, glanced at her stockings and gave a little cry of dismay. "Oh, dear, another run. I'll be only a minute."

In her bedroom Rowena darted to the telephone. Webster might be dining at his club. To her relief he had just come in.

"It's Rowena, Webster. I want your help."

"It waits your command."

"Isn't there some way of learning why they want Newton in Suruk?"

"None I know of. As the invitation was from their ambassador, procedure demands that any amplification of it should come from him. And he has said he can't give us any details."

"Could the King really pay Newton a million dollars?"

"Easily. He's getting nearly two million a day from oil royalties.

It must have taken considerable moral strength for Newton to say no."

"Moral strength, my foot. It just indicates one of Newton's few weaknesses."

"What's that?"

"Newton has no money sense. He seems to dote on being poor. Don't laugh darling; I mean it. Can't you put some pressure on him?"

"I don't see how. You must understand the situation, Rowena. The Suruki Ambassador requested the State Department to help him meet an American private citizen. The State Department produced him, thereby balancing the diplomatic courtesy account. Private citizen Newton Bemis has every right to know why he's been invited. King Sajjid's determined silence precludes any further inquiry by us. Don't forget Suruk is an autocrat's kingdom and its ruler's whims must be taken very seriously."

"Have you told the Ambassador Newton isn't going?"

"No. But I've reported his decision to the Department. I imagine Dr. Hunain will be informed tomorrow morning. I'm sorry, dear."

"Wait a moment. Do we have CIA agents in Suruk?"

"Probably in the oil fields. And there may be contacts with the interior I don't know about."

"Then why can't Harvey Priest point out to Newton that any information he might pick up from the King could be very valuable to the United States. I suggested Harvey to make it easier for you. If he agrees with you but doesn't want to urge Newton himself, then you can tell Newton the pressure came from upstairs."

There was a pause.

"Where can I telephone you later?"

"We're dining at Mandy Whitaker's. I want her to tell her two hundred newspapers how wonderful Newton is."

"Rowena, why do you stay in private life?"

"Because in my heart I'm just a homebody. Good-bye, darling."

When he telephoned Priest, Webster was surprised to learn that the Department, too, had been disconcerted by Newton's decision.

"Thank you, Harris," said Priest. "We were considering some tactful pressure."

"It's for Mr. Bemis," said Amanda Whitaker's maid. "The State Department is calling."

Newton put down his coffee cup and was led to the privacy of his hostess' study.

"Forgive me for disturbing you, Mr. Bemis," apologized Priest, "but it's a matter of some urgency. We've been told you don't want to go to Suruk."

Newton re-explained why.

"The Department appreciates your reluctance. Mr. Harris says that because he shared your feeling he didn't ask you to consider the invitation further."

"That's right."

"Before we report your decision to Dr. Hunain, may I discuss it a moment?"

Newton listened. Priest's argument ended with: "The Arabian temperament can be volatile at times so we are not too disturbed by Sajjid abruptly halting his national reform program. But we are concerned about what the Russians might be doing behind Sajjid's back. Wexford Drench, the King's friend and occasional advisor, is utterly reliable in what little he tells the British Ambassador and ours, and he says Sajjid up to now has declined all Russian tenders of assistance and communicates with the Russians in the legation quarter no more than with the Westerners. His only friendly gesture to the Soviets has been to permit a few Russian botanists to study with native authorities in a Suruki research station somewhere in the north. Drench says they are interested only in experiments on forage grasses that might one day improve the world's agronomy. The Russian Ambassador has told Drench he hopes their findings will strengthen Suruk's friendship with the Soviets.

"This may be quite true. But it's also possible that Sajjid has not fully informed Drench of all his foreign activities. We'd like more assurance that the botanists represent the only axe Moscow is grinding, so your being in personal contact with the King for only a day or two might be invaluable to us."

"Does the King speak English?"

"We're told he can make himself understood."

Newton promised to reconsider.

On their way back to N Street, Rowena tactfully allowed Newton to broach the subject of his telephone call.

"The State Department thinks I should go to Suruk. The Undersecretary put it in terms of patriotism."

"Oh. And what did you tell him, darling?"

"That I'd speak with Mr. Thackaray. They're getting some conclusions on tektites now and—"

"Tektites?"

"Bits of stone, about the size and shape of chocolate drops. They're found here, in Asia, almost everywhere. They were once liquid matter. If they're from the moon they can boost our lunar knowledge enormously. I've been assembling a report on our own research and I'd like to complete it before I do anything else."

"Maybe you could finish it in Suruk."

"I wouldn't like to chance it."

"When do they want you to leave?"

"Day after tomorrow."

"Maybe you can finish it by then."

"Perhaps. If I went I might not be back in time for the Chevy Chase party."

Rowena kissed him. "You mustn't give it another thought." What a wonderfully satisfactory husband he was going to be!

Ormond Fannestock had said he was leaving for Ceylon Monday. Tomorrow she would tell him some more of her requirements.

Chapter 5

"And these?" asked Newton. He pointed to five canvas bags on the floor beside the desk in Harvey Priest's office. Each bore the U.S. Mint stencil reading "MT 100."

"Maria Theresa dollars. They'll be in your luggage when you arrive and it's possible you'll find use for them. You won't be obliged to spend a penny for anything, but these can be handy for *baksheesh* and other disbursements. Maria Theresas have an authority all their own throughout Arabia. Ten are considered lordly tips for household servants.

"This is the name of the embassy attachée who will make the trip with you. You'll meet her at Kennedy Airport." The calling card read *Mrs. Zahra Haruba, The Embassy of His Majesty Sajjid ibn Mohammu al-Gamil ibn Quatahn.* "She was the private secretary of Sajjid's father and will supply any secretarial help you need. On the plane she'll brief you on court etiquette and whatever she knows about the King and his subjects. I've met her several times and she's a bright and chipper old party. Webster says you'll be pleased to learn she plays chess.

"Here's your schedule. As you'll leave Kennedy at eight, the airline hopes you'll have dinner on board. They're installing bedrooms for you and Mrs. Haruba, so you should be able to sleep before you arrive in Rome at ten A.M. The two-hour wait there is necessary for checking and refueling. The Alitalia manager says the flight to Suruk might be made in less than the time indicated so you can consider the three and a half hours as a maximum. That will put you down in Qam at approximately ten-thirty P.M."

Newton squinted at the mimeographed sheet.

"Puzzled?" asked Priest. Newton looked up and smiled.

"I was for a moment. Even with a two-hour time difference, a three-and-a-half-hour flight from Rome would put our arrival at five-thirty. I assume the 'Q.t.' after the '10:30' means Qam time."

"That's right. In some parts of Arabia the day begins at sunset. Therefore, the one on which you arrive will end about seven-thirty, Greenwich reckoning. Before you land the navigator will help you set your watch. At first it's a bit puzzling to recognize sundown as midnight. Suruk's clocks are adjusted on Fridays to the weekly differential in suntime."

"Fridays?"

"Yes. That's the Muslim Sunday. Care for an aspirin?"

Newton grinned. "Better send me a carload."

Priest picked up a slender pamphlet. "Here's another Arabic glossary. It's not as comprehensive as the one in your bag but it fits easily into a pocket.

"That about does it. If we learn anything useful before you leave we'll telephone you. If something comes in afterward, Briscoe will pass it on to you in Qam. Best of luck. Have a good time."

Newton emerged from the State Department building still mentally filing Priest's admonitions.

Rowena was waiting at the wheel of her sports car.

"All set?"

"If I can remember what I've been told. I know I won't forget where the top officials lunch. When I arrived, the receptionist said Priest was with the Secretary and would meet me in the restaurant. Somebody in the elevator told me the restaurant was on the fifth floor. I asked for Mr. Priest at the door and was told he hadn't come yet. About ten minutes later a search party found me. It seems there's a comparatively small-potato Mr. Priest who eats with his fellow underlings in the fifth-floor restaurant. The Powers have their own dining room on the eighth."

Rowena turned the car toward National Airport. Newton's plane to New York would not leave for almost an hour so they drove slowly through Rock Creek Park.

"Did you know it's costing King Sajjid fifty thousand dollars to fly you to Suruk?" Newton stared. "It's true. Bill Whiting found out for me."

"Who's Bill Whiting?"

"He handles transportation for the Senate. The Alitalia people told him that's the per diem rate for a DC-8. It seems the King wasn't certain when you'd like to leave and preferred chartering the plane on a twenty-four hour basis to booking it for a single flight. That way, taking you to Suruk would have cost only about thirty thousand dollars. Isn't it nice to have a host who doesn't pinch pennies?"

"He hasn't stopped there," reported Newton numbly. "The King is having the runway at Qam extended half a mile. The dryer and lighter air in Arabia obliges planes to land and take off at higher speed, so up till now nothing bigger than a Caravelle could come to Qam. How many people are breaking their backs so I won't have to change planes in Rome? What in God's name can he possibly want me for?"

"You promised to stop worrying about it, darling. Let's just be grateful for his sweet little wedding present." Newton looked at her blankly.

"Wedding present?"

"Your fee, darling! The King's million gives us our New York house."

A sharp pang made Newton conscious of his stomach. "Rowena —I—"

Now Rowena, too, seemed startled. She lessened the car's

speed almost to a crawl, and he saw her eyes, wide with uncertainty, questioning his. How could he tell her that King Sajjid's monetary offer had had no bearing on his journey? It was too bad to disappoint her, but she must be told one could not accept a million dollars blindly from anyone.

"We mustn't count on it, darling."

Rowena grasped the wheel more firmly. "Why not?"

"I might not earn it." He was relieved to notice the car picking up speed again.

Rowena's laugh was affectionately tolerant. "Of course you will, my scrupulous love. The King feels obligated to pay you if you stay only half an hour. It would be an unpardonable insult if you didn't let him."

Newton gently squeezed the trembling hand on the wheel. "Keep facing the road. I don't mean just for safety's sake. It's vital to some delicate work I'm doing."

"What's that?"

"Framing another picture of you. I don't have one with the wind and sun in your face."

Rowena checked her agitation and permitted him to study her perfections until they crossed the bridge leading to the airport.

"But you won't hurt the King's feelings, will you, darling?"

"I'll try not to."

He said it gently, but, Rowena sensed, determinedly. She resigned herself to a temporary postponement of pressure.

A sudden gust of wind sent her hair flying behind her. Newton's eyes were still memorizing her profile. Her forehead, he decided, would have appealed greatly to Botticelli.

The office cot on which Newton had found a few hours sleep each night during the development of the Prometheus heat shield was again made ready for his use. After thirty hours of consultations with other Thackaray scientists, lengthy deductions from laboratory analyses, correlations of meteorological reports, and the dictation of his conclusions on tektites, the cot was still unused.

He dismissed the last battery of weary stenographers and returned to his flat in time to pack hastily and arrive at Kennedy International Airport in an airline limousine twenty minutes before the jet's departure. Exhilarated by the satisfaction of a task completed and six carefully spaced dosages of 10-milligram amphetamine pills, he felt as alert and wakeful as a man newly risen from a refreshing sleep.

Mrs. Haruba was small, chic, and, despite her gray hair, youthful looking at seventy. She had not hesitated to disclose her age when Newton, shortly after they had met in the Alitalia V.I.P. room at the airport, confessed he was not yet thirty. Newton liked her immediately. Her dark, intelligent eyes were as friendly as her smile was bright and eight years' residence in America had left only the faintest trace of a Near Eastern accent.

Promptly on schedule the plane glided into position for take-off. Five minutes later it was climbing above the coastal clouds. The sudden disclosure of a moon beginning to wane prompted Mrs. Haruba to exclaim, "You could not arrive in Qam more opportunely. Tomorrow night will be the last on which you can see the *Janayin Billail,* the Gardens of Beautiful Deceit, at their best. Have you heard of them?"

"No, but I like their name."

"I believe they are the only gardens in the world designed for enjoyment by moonlight. Two nights from now they will no longer be in full flower. But all Suruk is beautiful in the late spring. Perhaps the King will take you with him to the plateaus in the west. That is where most of Suruk's flowers are grown. They are sheltered from the Saudi winds by the high reaches of the *Jibal Himaye,* the Mountains of Protection. A fortnight from now one of the watchers stationed at the snow line will fire a gun to announce that he has seen the baby crescent of the new moon. With that the month of Shawwan officially begins and the next morning the King will set forth on his annual visit.

"Perhaps the rural roads have been widened since I last saw them. But in the days of King Sajjid's father they were so narrow that from a distance the approaching royal automobiles looked like boats moving through a sea of wild flowers, waves of grape hyacinths, poppies, and daffodils slapping at their wheels. Soon every car would be submerged in color, under rugs of flowers tossed on them by villagers as tokens of their welcome. If the King still follows tradition, he'll judge pageants of camels, some painted like giraffes, and burros, robed and festooned head to tail with flowers, giving prizes for the most ingenious designs. There will also be parades of children wearing garments of every color imaginable woven from buds and blossoms, sometimes fashioned from the petals of blue Persian lilies fastened to netting by honey paste. Often the older children carry portraits of the King, also made of flowers. There will be a night of festivities and the next morning the visit will end with prayers at the birthplace of Sajjid's great-grandfather, who established the present dynasty. Throughout Suruk at the same hour—it is called the Morning of Gratitude—Sajjid's people everywhere will be praying and thanking God for the birth of Sajjid the First.

"Almost all Suruki are deeply religious, partly because they're certain that they live on the actual site of the Garden of Eden. And since God allowed their ancestors to return to the most fertile soil in the world, each generation must prove itself worthy of its inheritance.

"They see God's favor in the fact that Suruk has been independent since the days of Zenobia. Our surrounding mountains have always discouraged invasion by land, and no enemy has ever been able to get a foothold on the coast. Until a century ago, the pirate states on the Gulf occasionally sent sea raiders, but they were always slaughtered in such numbers that they finally gave up trying."

"You mentioned Zenobia. Was Suruk part of her empire?"

"Yes. In A.D. 268, when Zenobia was Roman mistress of the East, she came to Qam on a royal visit. She was so impressed by its floriculture that she sent her own gardeners from Palmyra to study there. The superb quality of Suruki sheep prompted her to take home several for breeding purposes. The grass in the Palmyrene meadows was good for native flocks, but the importations soon lost their superiority. Zenobia and her herdsmen did not know that our grazing land is in low country near salt marshes. This and the fact that the fruits of trees Zenobia had had transplanted from Suruki soil were less delicious than those she had tasted here caused her to declare, 'The land of Suruk rests in the palm of God's hand and should not be subject to any earthly power.' Through the centuries the few foreigners who have also been permitted to sample Suruk's bounty have lamented that the rest of the world must be deprived of it."

"Can't your fruits be exported?"

"Unhappily, no. For several years an English botanist in Suruk experimented with some of the hardier fruits like our sweet lemons, asal oranges, and tangors. Their exportation might have helped our country's economy in the pre-oil days. The results were so discouraging that in reporting one failure to the King he wrote, 'I am almost convinced that a law of nature requires that the fruits of Eden be eaten in Eden.'

"Since the coming of modern refrigeration, attempts have been made to disprove the botanist's assumption, but even when shipped by air something in the genes of our vegetables and fruits causes them to spoil almost immediately."

Newton smiled. "Suruki oil seems to travel without damage."

"True, but knowing Suruk's past I sometimes wonder whether it will prove a blessing or a curse."

"Doesn't it depend on how wisely its earnings are employed?"

"How can one predict what greed and envy might do to a people with a history of conflict among themselves? Within its own borders Suruk has not always been peaceful. The Arabian saying that one goes to war for love, water, and roads has often been confirmed by our feuding tribes. Through the years *sheikh* after *sheikh* would usurp the throne and his family's rule would continue until it died out or was overthrown. A hundred years ago we had one of the cruelest rulers in our history. In Qam you can still see his palace. It is known as the House of the Spike. On the street side, victims of his displeasure would be nailed to the door and left to die. A distinguished judge denounced the King for his inhumanity and was himself stripped of his clothes, painted red, and facing backward, lashed to a camel and led through the streets to his execution. As they passed the judge's house, his daughter threw herself from the balcony in protest to the dishonor. The judge's son, who was a religious scholar, left his studies to organize a successful rebellion and was made king. He was Sajjid the First. He abolished all oppressive laws and inaugurated an era of peace and good will. Local wars over the toll rights of roads were ended by his making all roads subject to the Crown. The taxes of the villages that helped maintain them were reduced, the rights to waterways equitably allocated, and crimes of passion were greatly reduced by the strict enforcement of Muslim laws. The production of opium was no longer tolerated; its possession automatically incurred the death penalty, and the mistreatment of slaves was stopped. His reforms are still in force today."

The Italian steward, who had been waiting for an opportunity to interrupt, offered dinner menus. The printed selection included dishes of the Middle East. Mrs. Haruba answered Newton's question about one of them.

"*Chello kebab* is really Iranian, but it has its Suruki counterpart. It is made of broiled strips of marinated lamb that have been soaked overnight in yogurt mixed with onions and saffron. That is the kebab part. The *chello* is a mound of rice mixed with egg yolk and sprinkled with sumac."

Newton decided to welcome it as another international accent of a dinner that would include Iranian caviar, *consommé à la Bohémienne,* an Italian salad, and *fraises du bois.* As a patriotic fortification for the feast, he accepted the steward's suggestion of a second American martini.

"You will be able to enjoy many American dishes in Qam," said Mrs. Haruba. "I know they have been served when the King entertained in the legation quarter. The major domo in the palace there is now more familiar with Western tastes than he was a year ago. At the King's first dinner to your ambassador, he thought he was following American convention by putting a box of corn flakes at each place. Fortunately, the error was discovered before the guests arrived."

Mrs. Haruba lowered her voice as if fearing eavesdroppers and continued playfully, "I shall tell you a secret. Yesterday the Embassy sent several kinds of frozen foods which might be unobtainable in the oil-port markets so you will have almost everything you wish. Of course, you will be invited to enjoy Suruki food, too."

"I've had a little briefing on Arabian table manners," said Newton. "I'm told one serves oneself by reaching into each dish with the right hand."

"You are correct," said Mrs. Haruba. "And it's not quite so messy as it sounds, because after each service your hand is washed in rose water. There is one thing you must not fail to remember. If a dinner follows tradition, one of the dishes will be sheep's eyes. And no matter how your host urges you, it is considered discourteous if you take more than one handful."

The pimento-stuffed olive in Newton's cocktail glass seemed to be staring at him.

"I'll try to remember," he said.

Chapter 6

The revelry that filled every night of *Ramadan* had finally quieted and Qam was resting briefly under its multitude of stars. (More numerous over Qam, everybody knew, than any other place in the world.) A transient breeze brought rumors of the morning to the doves under the eaves of Ameen Abban's coffee house. One flew out to make sure. Eastward someone was extinguishing the festive colored lamps that outlined the great mosque, but the rim of the sky was still deep indigo. The dove glided back and murmured reassurance to its companions. Simultaneously Ameen Abban's wife, still a bit giddy from the forbidden *arak* she had drunk with her snoring husband, rose and before making her way to the well behind the house threw a street veil across her face. The strangers her husband had permitted to stay overnight in the coffee shed might have awakened. Both were asleep. Their white *thobes* and *ghutras* were like those many Suruki men wore. But the dirtiness of the *thobes* implied they had traveled far and it was hard to believe that the new *ghutra*s were the habitual head covers of either the thin, fox-like face or the one with fat cheeks and huge coarse lips. They were not Qamini. Perhaps they were pearlers from Marbhein. Pearlers were a mixed breed and some-times spawned monsters like these.

From the bottom of the street, the general quiet was broken by the kettledrum and gong of the *musahhir,* who cried as he did daily during *Ramadan,* "God give everyone a happy morning," thus informing wakened sleepers that they must eat their last meal of the day. In an hour it would be light enough to see the difference between white threads and black, after which one de-nied oneself all food and drink until the threads again became indistinguishable at nightfall.

Mrs. Abban, having cooled her thirst, shook off her drowsiness and went to the kitchen. She poured some of the coffee beans that had been roasting overnight into a brass mortar and began break-ing them with its pestle. The cheerful ringing quickened the wak-ening of her husband. He soon joined her in preparing for the morning's business, mixing some of the beans with powdered cardamom, some with cloves and others with saffron. His clients liked different flavors. By the time he had stuffed the long spouts of the coffee pots with fresh fibers for straining, Hassan and Achmed Jaras, two elderly brothers who lived next door, finished their breakfast and, bringing their waterpipe with them, took their usual places on the bench in front of the coffee house. As they had been Abban's patrons for years, they shouted through the doorway, *"Yalla!"* which means "Get going."

They were not really in a hurry. Both were former businessmen with nothing to do until the first call to prayer. Hassan had been a gunsmith, Achmed a highly respected slave dealer. Achmed had retired eight years ago when the present King's decree forbade the further importation of slaves, white or black. After they had their coffee, Quasim, the barber, would arrive to trim their beards and give them their fortnightly staining with henna.

Ameen Abban came from the house. As he was stylish he twice tinkled the cups against the pot before serving his spiciest coffee. He asked Hassan Jaras if his grandson had returned from his emergency duties on the airstrip.

"Not yet," replied his customer. "But when his mother brought him food last night he told her the work would be finished today before the second prayer."

"Why is the King determined to have it done so quickly? Is the Lament about to end?"

"One can only guess. My grandson heard a rumor that the King of Iran is coming for a visit and that it would be disgraceful if he saw that our landing place was shorter than the one in Teheran."

Baba, the *sous* seller, approached rattling his metal mugs against the copper jar from which he dispensed ice cold licorice-root juice. He, too, must make the most of the next hour. Yet he paused to share the gossip of the coffee drinkers and their host.

"I heard the Lament is ending and a great cloud of airplanes are arriving today with the Western luxuries we have been promised," Baba contributed.

Ameen Abban snorted. "I will believe I have a refrigerator when I see it by the light of those electric lamps that are still to come."

"You are an impatient man," said Baba. "The King has promised that everything good for us will arrive in time."

"Like the schoolhouse?" scoffed Ameen Abban. There was an embarrassed silence because of Ameen's boldness. The schoolhouse tragedy was not publicly discussed. Even Baba, who usually talked more than anyone, held his tongue. Hassan Jaras spoke. "The King wants assurance that there will be no more accidents. You are impatient, Ameen. It is only six months since the Period of Lament began."

Baba could keep quiet no longer. He glared at the coffee seller. "For a year almost all taxes have been abolished. You should be grateful."

"What is the use of having money if one cannot spend it on the good things of life?"

"I pity you for your discontent, but God give you prosperity," said Baba amiably. He moved on rattling his metal mugs and Ameen Abban went into the house.

As the brothers sipped their coffee, they speculated on the cause for the resumption of communication with the outside world. Did it mean the King was now certain there would be no more disasters such as the one which had brought the Program to a stop? The schoolhouse was to have been the first of many buildings which would alter the appearance of blessed Qam. The physical changes had begun with the broadening of the streets leading to the schoolhouse site from the *Bab el Shem,* the most eastern of Qam's six gates, and the widening of the portals of the gate, itself, to admit trucks bringing building material from the new airport.

They remembered the day the population had gathered about the Blue Mosque to hear the Chief Imam ask God's tolerance on the unbelievers engaged on the Project, and the King's edict that the school's completion was to be followed by the creation of a great hospital, a radio station, a cinema, a food-freezing plant, and other innovations. His subjects were told that through the money paid the King by the oil company, they would have many benefits enjoyed in the rich Western nations.

In the new schoolhouse, during the mornings and afternoons, children would receive instruction in the books of the Koran, the four operations of arithmetic, and other elementary studies. Every night there would be classes for adults. Two weeks after its completion all the children in the afternoon classes had been dismissed for the day, save thirty. They were detained to learn a poem to be recited a few days later when the King made his first visit to the school. Without warning, the poorly constructed walls collapsed, killing everyone in the room. Among the children was one of the King's sons, the young Prince Jahaur.

In the grief-stricken city the Chief Imam declared that the disaster was an evidence of God's displeasure. Without comment the King proclaimed an indefinite Period of Lament. Except in the oil fields, all motor transportation throughout Suruk was banned.

The few owners of Suruk's first jeeps, trucks, and farm machinery resigned themselves to the re-employment of camels and other draft animals. Most of the Suruki who had radio sets obeyed orders not to use them. The few who didn't soon found them useless because one could not buy new batteries. Outside Suruk, the country's suddenly resumed isolation was attributed to the eccentricity of a ruler with a fourteenth-century mind. Within the kingdom, the vast majority of the population having not yet learned of the existence of motor-driven vehicles for their fields or vacuum cleaners for their homes continued to live their placid lives in the manner of their ancestors. Among the tribes in the north, some *sheikhs,* incensed on learning they were not to surround themselves with promised luxuries, seethed embarrassingly until Sajjid sent assurances that the deprivations would exist only for the duration of the Lament. In Qam a preponderant fealty to their sovereign was reflected in the fatalistic readiness of the brothers Jaras to accept whatever might result from the airport's activity.

On this twentieth day of *Ramadan,* in the sixth month of the Lament, most of those grieved by the deaths of the school children were reconciled to their loss. Once again Qam was fasting by day and feasting by night, its gates still firmly closed against the invasion of modernity. The grumblings of the Ameen Abbans with their smuggled pictures of TV sets and deep freezes were not loud enough to disturb the city's ancient tranquility.

In the shed, Ameen Abban cautiously awakened his two lodgers and pressed a finger to his mouth, lest they talk loudly. The warning was unnecessary. Neither spoke as their host placed before them sweet tea, pancake-like bread, and slices of melon. He had been told to feed them well. As the men began to eat, Ameen Abban returned to the house. He filled his own mouth with *khat* leaves, pulled from a branch in the kitchen, and went to the street to refill the Jaras brothers' cups. Ameen Abban liked publicly to evidence respectability and as even *khat* was forbidden during fasting hours, chewing the delicious leaves now was a last indulgence before dawn. The arrival of the barber halted the brothers' conjecturing about a faint sound they had just heard on a distant street. It suggested the rumbling of a motor truck. The barber said no sound of a truck had reached his ears. Last night, however, he had received news which the arrival of a motor truck would tend to confirm. The brothers sat stiffly on their bench as the barber unstrapped his equipment. Everyone knew he belonged to Qam's anti-Program minority which wanted no change in its old pattern of life. Had his customers been informed that the Lament was about to end, and that the shrine of the sacred Khidr was to be supplanted by a Christian church for the use of foreigners who would arrive soon to rebuild the city? In one breath, both brothers said they believed the report was without foundation. The barber worked for a while in silence, and the brothers engaged themselves with virtually the same thoughts. Before the Program had been halted, both had regretfully observed the appearance of religious intolerance, common enough in other Arab countries but hitherto absent from Suruk. The great majority of Suruki had never seen a foreigner. Those who had worked with the King's friend, *Ustaz* Drench, had never regarded him as representing a religion inimical to their own. It would be a pity should the Program be revived if the mere presence of Christians increases the heat of implacable resistance.

"What the hell is he up to?" asked the assistant to the foreman of the ASOCO maintenance crew from Batrul Mina. Three days ago they had suddenly been assigned to reactivate the Qam airport where a major runway was being hastily lengthened.

"He's overhaulin' the harem. He don't want the babes he's importin' to be put on a shuttle at Batrul and maybe try to escape."

"No clowning, Dave. Why?"

"Wouldst that I knowed. But he ain't written to me in over a week. I know that this mornin' they're lettin' some trucks into Qam with gasoline and oil for the royal garages."

"Maybe he's come out of his shell again."

"That I cannot say. But you're gonna land in the royal tank if they catch you drinkin' that beer. Better do it in the hangar office."

The bells of Qam vary greatly in their voices and personalities. The most somber and resounding is *Jabas Allah,* the Father of Bells, which is in the tower above the Great Gate. It was hung there centuries ago to warn Qamini of approaching enemies. Today, when great mallets covered with leather produce notes deep and grave, *Jabas Allah* informs the King's subjects that edicts are about to be proclaimed. There are the dull, impersonal bells with which leaders of funeral processions demand respectful attention for the dead. They are presumed to set the key for the singing of the children who precede the mourners, but they never do. Thus they seem discordant and indifferent to grief. The most unpleasant bells are the strident, nervous clamorers one hears after nightfall which inform those within the city walls of late-comers without. The bells that hang from the necks of camels pulling vendors' carts clank rather than ring, but they are soft and rather pleasant, especially to those who, hearing them, know they need not carry home baskets of charcoal or salt blocks from the dealers in the *suqs.* The gayest bells, at least those which become most feverishly excited, are intertwined with dried goats' hooves and circle the waists of the timekeepers at the slaves' clubs. They are heard only on Fridays in vacant courtyards where slaves and ex-slaves gather for recreation. Against plaintive threnodies from six-stringed harps, the bells' merry chirps and the clicks of the castanet-like hooves as their wearers leap in the air set the rhythm for the chanting of songs as old as the genes in the blood of those who hear them.

Surely the gentlest bells in all Qam murmur in the gardens of the rich when currents of air urge them to perform. Each sends forth its own distinct tremor of pleasure. The sweetest sing in King Sajjid's Garden of the New Day. Each of the gardens about the Great Palace has individuality; some are fantastically ingenious, some august and splendid, others seasonally functional. But none is so fragrant in the early morning as the Garden of the New Day. Equally superlative are its bells. Small windflowers of sound, they hang in clusters of crystal and silver from the fruited branches of a pomelo tree.

The breeze which had poked its nose into the eaves of Ameen Abban's coffee house tired of scuttling through streets and alleyways and decided to refresh itself in the clean smells about the Great Palace. Now it began to jostle playfully whatever was moveable in the pomelo tree and from crystal and silver throats came notes delicate and charming, small delights that crossed the sleeping garden, floated through the window of Sajjid's bedchamber and stirred him to wakefulness.

Hearing his master moving about, the slave Jabil, who was also named the Mat because his duty was to sleep outside the King's bedroom door, opened it. After receiving Sajjid's blessing he returned to the hall and signaled a waiting valet that their master was awake.

Even during *Ramadan* no Moslem is required to worship God before the first official call to prayer. Yet as soon as he had bathed Sajjid fell to his knees in thankfulness for the recent favors God had shown him. Today the wonderful young man from America would arrive. Last night Uncle Wex had agreed that from what was known of Mr. Bemis' character he might be able to counsel Sajjid wisely on his plans for Suruk's future. Certainly he could be trusted with the secret of secrets which up to now Sajjid had shared only with Uncle Wex. Uncle Wex agreed with him that because, when a youth, Mr. Bemis had been familiar with all the machinery in the secret room, he could, on learning how Sajjid intended to employ it, give invaluable advice. God had also favored him in causing Uncle Wex to visit him at such an opportune time, his affection for Sajjid undiminished. Now that the storm in Sajjid's mind was completely over and Uncle Wex was back in the palace for the first time since Jahaur's death, it was appropriate that Uncle Wex's appearance occasioned the ending of the Lament.

When Uncle Wex had first come to Suruk, Sajjid believed the knee he was forever climbing was that of a real uncle. Uncle Wex's wife had, of course, been called aunty because all women in the palace other than his mother and the servants were called aunts. As Sajjid grew older, Uncle Wex had become a living book, containing all there was to know about things that grew from the earth and the creatures that moved on the ground or in the air. Sajjid had been thirty-seven when his father died eight years ago and his heart welled with gratitude when Uncle Wex said he would stay in Suruk and help Sajjid be a worthy king.

Sajjid thanked Allah once more for having poured cooling memories of Uncle Wex into his mind to check the scalding rage against all things into which the news of Jahaur's death had plunged him. It had followed many errors for which he could blame no one but himself. Even now the recognition of them burned his conscience like fire. The greatest was of course his rejection of the oil company's advice on Suruk's rebirth. The advisors they had sent him had worked in good faith, and it was his overestimation of the astuteness of his own officials that had allowed swindlers to have a hand in putting up the school building. In the fury of his grief he he decreed the death of the villains responsible for the flimsiness of the structure. When told they had fled the country, he had been prompted to have Uncle Wex killed for failing to detect their duplicity. Before he could issue the command, God had checked his frenzy and made him recognize that Uncle Wex had had nothing to do with the cause of the tragedy. Completing his prayers, Sajjid expressed his thanks for the first demonstration of ASOCO's good will. The moment the wells on the coast had become productive, the company had sent men to install modern plumbing, electric lighting, and telephones in the palace.

Sajjid rose. He must not delay much longer the appointment of a successor among his sons. Should he relent in his rigid *sukut* against his third son, Musallim? Musallim for Khaiyir? Khaiyir had been the brightest of them all and in his young years had truly merited the title of His Beneficence. If there were time before Mr. Bemis' arrival, he would summon Musallim and if the young man showed remorse for his defections, he might end the silence between them imposed by the *sukut* and allow himself and his son again to be on speaking terms. He must also try to find a moment for Farha. He hoped her heart was light and that she was happy over her approaching marriage. Next to Jahaur, she had been the most endearing of all the palace children, and, according to her mother, had not been spoiled by her years abroad. He went into the garden to inhale its scents. He stopped before the unique flowering cereus his father had planted. The palace gardeners insisted the blue of its flowers was as deep as it had been last year. When it was light enough he would look at it again and ask Uncle Wex for his opinion.

Jabil the Mat quietly opened the bedroom door. The King had finished his prayers and was feeling the young fruit of the smaller apricot tree. Jabil closed the door and signaled the valet in the hall to bring the King his breakfast.

Nuri, the *douidar,* was blaming himself for wakening Professor Drench. Of course it wasn't the sound of his blowing into the sand pipe that had done it. Those particles of sand which the pipe caused to strike small fruits without bruising them were soundless and the routed birds made no more protest than when quarreling among themselves. Nuri assumed what had brought the old man to the window was his shout of triumph after four bulbuls and a bee eater had simultaneously been pelted away. Nuri liked Professor Drench and hoped he had not offended him. When you are ten years old and the son of a palace slave you might get more than a severe scolding for waking a nonbeliever who had no need to be up this early.

"Good morning, Nuri," said Wexford Drench cheerfully, his eyes on the waking sky. "May God give you a day filled with light."

"The same to you!" yelled Nuri in effect. Everything was fine.

The professor had not even been annoyed. As he did not often have such an opportunity, Nuri decided to continue the conversation. "Our guest from America—he is coming today?"

"This evening, Nuri." On the hill a mile beyond the palace wall Drench saw the night lights still burning about the shrine of Khidr. When Sajjid had first consulted his ASOCO advisors, they had said the hill was unquestionably the best site for the radio tower. Now that Sajjid was himself again he would undoubtedly have their advice followed. The Chief Imam was among those prejudiced against the entire Program and as Khidr, the saint of childless women, was highly revered, the Imam would again be prompted to howl about sacrilege. Sajjid had had to impose his authority as Suruk's religious head to obtain the Chief Imam's public tolerance of the Program's inception. He had been reported secretly exultant when it was arrested. Last night Sajjid had hinted that the Chief Imam would be replaced by a less austere prelate. It would be a risk because, despite his dogmatic obstinacy, the Chief Imam was popular. It was a risk Sajjid seemed to feel he must take. God grant he had made it after due reflection.

Sajjid had not yet overcome his penchant for hasty decisions. The possibility of Mr. Bemis' being able to contribute useful advice had not been considered for five minutes when Sajjid had begun his overtures to Washington. If it proved to be an error it would, of course, not be a grievous one, entailing merely a waste of time and money. His private qualms were diminishing in his own contemplations of the American's visit. The extraordinary Mr. Bemis might even more than justify its costs. Unless extrasensory perception were among his talents he would of course have no knowledge of Sajjid's personality and temperament. On the plane Mrs. Haruba had no doubt been feeling it her duty to extol Sajjid's benevolence. From her fulsomeness, a perceptive Bemis might suspect that her royal master ruled his people by intimidation. A few words with Bemis privately would clear the air of possible misconception. Bemis must be told that while he might observe occasional indications of headstrong childishness, Sajjid was essentially a faithful steward of his country's welfare, as free from corruption as his father had been and as instinctively generous. If only Sajjid could learn to weigh his impulses, he could be the duplicate of his wonderful father. How warm his welcome to them had been when almost fifty years ago Lucy, his bride, and he had arrived by camel train from Marbhein and were taken by astonished guards to an equally astonished king. When they had told him they had learned Arabic in order to study eighteenth- and nineteenth-century Near Eastern manuscripts in the British Museum, he had clasped Drench in his arms and invited the young couple to consider his palaces their homes. Every facility would be theirs for studying what had brought them to Qam. Butterflies were Lucy's principal concern, Drench's the flora of Suruk.

Ten years later, the roots of their affection now sunk deep in its soil, Suruk had become their home and its king their dearest friend. In his memory as well as for Sajjid's sake, he must do his best to see that Suruk emerged as painlessly as possible into the modern world. The process needed all the help Drench, Bemis, or anyone else could give. The constant flow of oil wealth was flooding the royal treasury. The living descendants of a people which for two thousand years had depended almost entirely on an agrarian economy were both feverish and frightened by the approach of change. The simple-minded were either rapaciously greedy for novelties or fanatically threatening with denouncements of every proposed improvement; there were rumors of secret meetings of dissidents, dedicated to blocking the Program with their lives. The intelligent, though sympathetic, were also alarmed. Would the Program, they asked, bring new life to Mother Suruk's veins? Or would it make her one with Ma'in, the once great city of Wadd, the Father God of the Moon, now mere rubble in the desolate empty quarter of Saudi Arabia. The months of cessation had provided time for him to study as intelligently as he could the Program's revision. Today there was no doubt that Sajjid relied on him to help see it through. Drench's eyes went to a grave in the garden and his heart to Lucy's abiding presence. "I am so ignorant of things

I should know. Lucy, you must be with me now more than ever."

Drench lifted his eyes from the garden and looked south. Even this early one could see the outlines of the fruiteries. Once again they had justified the effort he and Lucy had put into them. The *xylomelium* experiments, five years of misses and near hits, had ended triumphantly. The problem had been to keep the pear from lignifying as it matured. For forty-eight hours the perfected fruit had retained its fleshiness. Moreover, its taste had been delicious and, at this moment, twelve hours after eating it, he felt extraordinarily fit. Was there some energizing property in its flesh?

Drench took out his watch. The hour of the first prayer was near. There was no longer time for contemplation. First he must write two letters; one to the chief pomologist at Kew, a second to his correspondent, Dr. Pierre Dansereau, at the New York Botanical Gardens. They would welcome the news of the new pear. Nuri's piping voice diverted him again.

"I am to be one of the dancers who will greet the foreigner. Would you like to see what I shall do?"

"I'll have to wait unless you want that honey creeper to gorge himself."

"Oh, that devil!" Opening his sand pouch Nuri raced toward a threatened nectarine. Drench felt a gentle flick at his heart, as the boy, despite his haste, skirted the flower-bordered grave where Lucy lay. The small rosebush behind the headstone needed trimming again. He would do it today himself.

"*Alla yihfazak*, Nuri," Drench called to the little boy.

Nuri cheerfully echoed that he hoped God would keep the professor safe. After the professor withdrew Nuri looked about for the ortolan which a few minutes earlier had been skulking audaciously about the young grapes. A flutter of wings behind him spun him around. It was Habibi, the Lady Farha's tiny parakeet, resting for a moment on a spray of jasmine. Habibi was always welcome. He never pecked at the fruit and often said things so funny you could not help laughing. Habibi repeated only what came from the lovely mouth of the Lady Farha. Sometimes you could not understand what he said because it was in one of the foreign tongues the Lady Farha knew. The Lady Farha had gone to school in a country called Sfeezerlaunt somewhere in Europe.

It was good to be a *douidar* and have the run of the palace and listen to the ladies and carry messages, things the eunuchs used to do before His Majesty ordered them out of service and gave their jobs to boys. But nothing had been more fun than being with the Lady Farha and hearing her sing and listening to her stories of Sfeezerlaunt. Last year when the Lady Farha had come back to Qam she had given Nuri a wonderful present. When he proved he could sing the verse of *Surlepahndaveenon* she had taught him, she rewarded him with a wonderful clock. Every hour a little door in the top of the clock opened and a bird came out, chirped, and withdrew into the clock behind the closing door. Nuri had had no opportunity to tell the Lady Farha that while investigating the machinery of the clock he had done something which caused the bird to stay on the other side of the door. Since she came back from Europe again last week, the Lady Farha had been with other ladies whenever he had seen her. On the few occassions on which she had left the harem, she had been wearing the heavy veil that indicated she was now engaged to be married.

Up in the harem quarters, the small parakeet flew in from the terrace and lighted on a pillow. An upthrown arm covered the small ear it had come to peck. After waiting a few moments for the arm to move, the parakeet was attracted by the brightness of a gilded photograph frame and flew across the room to perch on it. Then it hopped down to a silver pot of *kohl* which nestled among the several toilet bottles and looked at the figures in the photograph: a group of laughing girls at a Swiss ski run. Quickly bored, the bird flew back to the bed. The thwarting arm had moved enough to expose the lobe of the sleeper's ear. Habibi then enjoyed its daily prerogative, a nip, not painful, merely sufficient to pull the ear's owner from sleep.

"Bonjour, Bibi." murmured Farha's sleepy voice. The bird watched a slender arm stretch toward a glass of colored liquid on the breakfast tray beside the bed. The right hand holding the glass poured a few drops into the palm of the left. Habibi did not need the soft, "Here, little darling," to enjoy its morning ration of tangerine juice and some crumbled fragments of a sweet bun.

Having fed Habibi, Farha ate her own breakfast. Then she opened the curtains of the window nearest her bed and was startled. The sun had already risen above the Blue Mosque! She had only half heard Tagir, her mother's woman attendant, bringing in the tray before the Hour of the Threads and had gone back to sleep. How fortunate Mama was visiting Abdel Sadek's family. Mama would have considered eating this late an offense against God. She would also have thought it wicked for a daughter about to be married to sit up most of the night on the palace roof with the other ladies of the household. It was absurd to think that God would have found anything improper in her enjoying last night's fun. She had felt truly at home being with cousin Anissa, each pouring out her thoughts as they had done when they were children. Anissa had agreed that there could be nothing wrong in a bride-to-be enjoying the fireworks of the last week of *Ramadan* as she had been permitted to do when small. She could remember Aunt Lucy then saying that her husband had introduced them into Qam many years ago. Anissa had been astonished to learn that Christians did not celebrate their religious festivals with fireworks. In Lausanne, Tabby Proctor said that in her country they were best seen on a political holiday in July when the United States celebrated the nation's birthday anniversary. How Tabby would have enjoyed last night's gaiety, especially after the last rockets had filled the air with hissing silver snakes and exploding bouquets of red, blue, and golden lights, when with the stars and rising moon overhead she and Anissa had listened to the merrymaking in the streets and watched the great bowls of colored fires burning on hundreds of rooftops. Tabby would have recognized many of the songs sung last night by Aunt Cherifa and old Princess Saudah, songs sweet and sad which Farha remembered first hearing when she was very young. Farha had been persuaded to sing into Tabby's tape recorder. Tabby, who could eat anything, would have relished the midnight feast and enjoyed at least the pantomime of those famous women entertainers who were so popular among the harems of Qam that their services had to be engaged months ahead. They had convulsed everyone with their mocking skits about men and their absurdities. Nothing could have been funnier than the burlesque of the man who wanted to go to Beirut for a holiday but whose wives demanded that he bring them so many presents, he discovered he could not afford the journey. The only jibe she and Anissa had disliked was the one about the husband whose wife caught him in lies after giving her jewelry to a secret mistress. Most of the watchers had cried, "Lululu!" approvingly and laughed, but there had been cruelty and meanness in the husband's attitude. When the gaiety had at last come to an end, Anissa had been most helpful and encouraging in discussing Farha's impending marriage. Anissa pointed out that there was no reason to fear that Abdel Sadek would not be as kind and wonderful a husband as Anissa's had proved to be. As a Suruki official stationed at Batrul Mina, he had felt he should not leave his post, but had permitted Anissa to return to Qam for Farha's wedding. Anissa, too, had found herself betrothed to a man she had never seen, and perhaps she was right in assuming that Abdel Sadek, aware of and pleased by Farha's European schooling, would not expect her to accept the humiliating restraints usually imposed on Suruki wives. When she told Anissa of Mama's hint that her bridegroom might take her to Europe, Anissa said that indicated his liberation from Suruk's tradition and his desire to make Farha happy.

The voices of the *muezzins* in the city's minarets chanted:

> *Alahu akbar! Alahu akbar!*
> *Alahu akbar! Alahu akbar!*
> God is most great.
> I testify that there is no god but God.
> I testify that Muhammad is the Apostle of God.
> Come ye to prayer.

Come ye to salvation
Prayer is better than sleep.
God is most great.
There is no god but God.

Last week on the morning after her return from Switzerland, because of Mama's presence she had knelt and touched the ground with her head at the calls to prayer. The physical actions had been almost automatic and it had been rather pleasant to discover that she remembered and could repeat all the old prayers. But when four days ago Mama had gone to visit Abdel Sadek and his relatives, she had resumed the shorter, simpler prayers, the ones on Duty and Gratitude, which she had said at school when her Christian classmates were at chapel and she was alone in her room. Knowing what she did now about other religions, she could no longer believe that the God of All Things became unhappy when his children omitted some of the lengthy formalities of Muslim ritual. Now Farha felt no guilt in briefly but earnestly thanking God for the blessings He had given her and asking for strength to meet her coming obligations as a faithful wife. If Sadek were as liberal in his views as Mama said he was, surely he would only smile at the scrupulous piety of his mother-in-law.

In the shed behind the coffee house the strangers silently watched Ameen Abban take away the remains of their breakfast. A little later the calls of the *muezzins* stopped and all Qam was at prayer. The strangers decided to return to sleep. It would be several hours before someone came to secrete them in the palace.

Chapter 7

What was called the Leper Colony by its foreign residents was for centuries a delightful estate, six miles from Qam, where an air-cooled summer palace nestled in the center of a wide pleasance of gardens and gazelle runs. A year ago when Britain and the United States set up their embassies, King Sajjid had agreed with Uncle Wex that it would be gravely discourteous to make the new legations house themselves in Marhbein or the two oil ports so far from Suruk's capital city. Creating an enclave of embassies near the old summer palace would not impair the age-old seclusion of Qam itself.

Two swimming pools, two tennis courts, and two modern residences quickly sprang up. Before they were completed, Russia's insistent eagerness to honor Suruk by more than its consulate in Marhbein added a third ambassadorial household to the community, although Russia's trade with Suruk was virtually nonexistent.

As Britain and the United States still maintained their consular offices in Marhbein the duties of their ambassadors were few. And since the entire foreign colony was now denied access to Qam, the ambassadors' wives saw each other constantly and together made occasional shopping trips to Marhbein. Every day Natasha Voronsky, the wife of the Russian Ambassador, and her two small children were in and out of both swimming pools like seals. Natasha herself was perfecting a deadly service on the courts. Although her husband neither swam nor played tennis, when they first arrived he had encouraged Natasha to make the most of the companionship offered by the wives of his opposite numbers. But for the last six months as she and the children spent more and more time away from their official home he had grown less and less enthusiastic about her neighborliness. This morning only the presence of little Igor and Marina curbed his fury over her defection as a faithful Soviet wife.

"I have told you," contended Natasha coolly, "everything Dolly and Beryl know about him. He is simply a young scientist coming to advise the King on the modernization program."

"There is a liar under this roof." Voronsky turned toward his offspring. "Igor and Marina, go to the kitchen and tell the cook to sing you a song." Well-trained, the children descended from their chairs and left the room.

"I am not the fool you think me, Natasha," continued Voronsky. "I know all about Newton Bemis. The man is a missile designer undoubtedly coming to select sites in Suruk. Your increased association with our enemies has been attended by a decrease in reporting what might be vital bits of information. If your observation continues to dim, I shall confine your movements to the embassy grounds."

Natasha's eyes blazed warningly. "And will you try to convince Beryl and Dolly that I am sick?" she challenged. "They would not swallow such nonsense. There would be forceful inquiries to Drench and he would see to it that the King demanded your recall. And how do you think the war office would react to your bungling your job? I am not a fool either."

Soviet diplomats are required to be adept in fending off the incontrovertible. Natasha's husband smiled affectionately and attempted to press her hand to his lips.

"As you know, my darling, when I am disturbed, I bark but I do not bite. My statement was, of course, extravagant. However, my beloved, do try to be more helpful."

Why, the Ambassador asked himself, had he not listened to his classmates at the School of Political Science when they urged him to overcome his infatuation for Natasha Bruborowska? They had pointed out that, while attractive, she was a ballerina who would never achieve first rank. He had dismissed the disparagements as the ruses of competitors for her hand. It was bitter to recognize so belatedly that the warnings may have been offered in good faith. The woman had not been the prize he thought he had won. Her inability to make any distinction between official and personal relationships demonstrated a basic stupidity. Accepting her capitalist neighbors as trustworthy friends proved she was, even if unwittingly, a dangerous cryptoconcessionist. From now on none of his political operations must reach her ears. When he returned to Moscow he would get a divorce.

The Ambassador repaired to his study. It was maddening to have to depend on one stupid household slave for information on activities in the Qam palace. Were the British and American Embassies equally ignorant of the contents of that constantly locked room to which only the King and his British lackey had access? Surely both the other ambassadors had their own palace informants. Probably they shared the confidence of the English-born Drench. Had he told them what had been in the unmarked crates and boxes brought in a truck from Marbhein seven months ago? Did they know the identity of the two silent men, presumably technicians, who had arrived with the truck, supervised the carrying of the crates and boxes into the secret room, and silently left with the empty truck two days later?

Since then the stupid Jabil had reported nothing until three days ago. The information he then supplied had been infuriatingly meager. Passing the locked room Jabil said he had seen a large steel cylinder outside the door, put there to be disposed of with other palace refuse.

In his study, Voronsky unlocked his personal filing cabinet and carefully extracted a metal case. Until today it had contained only documents and several small specimens of as yet unanalyzed quartz discreetly gathered by Boyshekov on his latest visit to one of the anti-Sajjid *sheikhs* in the north. Voronsky turned the case on its left side before opening it. If unauthorized searchers forced its lid while it stood upright, the acid immediately released within would both destroy its contents and set off an explosive which would kill the examiner. From the case, he removed a small card. Typed on it was the lettering he had copied from a zinc tag now in Moscow. Before the rubbish collectors came to take the cylinder away Jabil had removed the tag from its neck. The tag read: "AJAX C. D." Voronsky again pondered deeply. Jabil said the cylinder weighed at least 60 kilos. If, as Voronsky conjectured, the contents of the secret room were models of missile parts waiting for Bemis to demonstrate, why had the cylinder been discarded?

Again he read the decoded message received this morning from Moscow: ZINC PLATE IDENTICAL WITH TAGS ATTACHED TO CONTAINERS OF CARBON DIOXIDE PRODUCED BY AJAX EQUIPMENT COMPANY OF PARAMUS NEW JERSEY. PARAMUS IS ADJACENT TO EXPERIMENTAL LABORATORY BRANCH OF GOWERTON CHEMICAL CORPORATION, KNOWN TO BE SUPPLYING SOLVENTS FOR MISSILE MATERIALS. REQUIRE DETAILED REPORTS ON ACTIVITIES OF NEWTON BEMIS FROM MOMENT OF ARRIVAL UNTIL DEPARTURE. IF RELIABLE PALACE INTELLIGENCE SOURCE UNOBTAINABLE, YOU WILL SUPPRESS PERSONAL EMOTIONS AND INSTRUCT MADAME V TO RECONSIDER HER RESISTANCE TO HIS BENEFICENCE'S OVERTURES. HER ACCEPTANCE WOULD BE RECOGNIZED AS HEROIC ACTION AND SUITABLY REWARDED.

Voronsky groaned. In Natasha's present mood it would be futile to attempt sending her into Qam for even the briefest period. And even if she were willing to go, what good would it do? The recent hints by His Beneficence that he was planning independent action to take over the throne had created a disquieting doubt of the man's fundamental reliability. Arab princelings were volatile creatures. It was even possible that the Americans or the British had undermined the Soviet's understanding with His Beneficence. They too might be scheming to acquire the minerals in the north. It could be disastrous if His Beneficence was now the Westerners' man. If only Boyschekov were here to give advice. But Boyschekov would be in the north for several days determining the flexibility of a possibly co-operative *sheikh* and completely out of reach. What could one man be expected to do here with only imbeciles around him?

Voronsky was seldom moved to consider the possibility that he had been a complete failure as a diplomat. He did so now. Briefly, but with such a release of inner pressure by great loud sobs that Natasha, about to knock on the door and seek to make peace, withdrew in disgust at her husband's ignoble self-pity.

In the British Embassy Sir Tertius Hipp left the breakfast table as soon as he decently could for the comparative coolness of the chancellery. Beryl's curiosity this morning was a bit trying. He had glanced at the headlines of the Beirut *Daily Star* and the Teheran *Journal,* two English language newspapers, the scanning of which he had made part of his daily duties, when Lady Hipp, still holding her napkin, appeared in the doorway. With effort she made herself heard above the rumble of the air conditioner.

"Puffin, there's another possibility!"

"What would that be?" Sir Tertius' eyes were still scanning the newspapers, a preoccupation he hoped would cause Beryl to be brief. Beryl possessed many admirable qualities, but, by God, she could try one's patience when she chattered on and on about something in which only she was interested.

"Maybe the great day is here! Not just one man, but hundreds of them, architects, engineers, doctors, educators, and . . ."

"Beryl!" Sir Tertius had to look up to gain her attention. "The revised Program hasn't been definitely approved. Eustace Drench has told us the Program will not resume until it is."

"But no one would be mad enough to add half a mile of tarmac to an abandoned runway merely because a perfectly healthy young man is arriving. Why couldn't he be shuttled to Qam from the company airport at Batrul Mina like anybody else? If it was Eustace's idea, it proves he's crackers."

"Nonsense, the old boy's as sane as Sunday. Yesterday he read me a page and a half he's just written on *lycaenae icari*. He has quite a sound theory on why the males and females have such different coloring. Made me wish I'd kept up my butterfly collecting when I was at Cheam."

"If he's no further than the letter 'L' he'll never live long enough to finish the book."

"I hope I have half his vigor when I'm seventy-four. He still plays damned decent tennis. And if the Yanks and Voronsky's chaps would only co-operate and learn cricket I wouldn't hesitate having Eustace play any position." He closed his eyes momentarily. "As I recall, when he was batsman for Harrow he scored five hundred eighty-eight in a seven-hour match spread over six afternoons."

That did it. As usual his clever introduction of cricket halted Beryl's conversational momentum. Lady Hipp glanced guardedly and saw her husband smiling vaguely at the ceiling. Yes, he was preparing to reminisce further.

"I'm sending Habeeb and Uluba into Qam," barked Lady Hipp. "Do you want anything from the *suqs?*"

Puffin floated back to earth and turned again to his newspapers.

"Have them buy some *aswad* ink. It's better for fountain pens than ours."

"Will do, dear." Lady Hipp fled. Puffin had no idea what a bloody bore he could be sometimes.

In his study, Thornton Briscoe put down the telephone. When he rejoined Dolly in the breakfast room, she was lifting her egg from the grill on the table. As she did so, there was a hissing burst of electric sparks from the toaster.

"Wouldn't you know," she moaned, "Ali Saif told me yesterday we have no more fuses."

"Maybe Beryl or Natasha can spare some."

"I hope so. I wouldn't relish another six-hour trip to Marbhein this week. What did Useless want?"

Before her husband could reply, there was another distracting sound; that of an approaching plane.

"He's ten hours early!" wailed Dolly, now ready for a full day of calamities.

She dashed to the window. A twin-engined Convair, a thousand feet overhead, was descending toward the royal airport.

"It's the control tower crew from Batrul Mina," said Briscoe from his chair at the table. "They weren't due for half an hour. Why are you so nervous?"

"There are so many things to do today. How long will the airport reception last, do you think?"

"About one minute as far as we're concerned."

Dolly almost dropped a spoonful of marmalade.

"What's happened?"

"Poor Eustace was quite embarrassed. The King had decided to be at the airport, himself, and have Bemis ride with him into Qam. I asked Drench if he'd like us not to be there. After all, Washington says Bemis isn't here officially. Drench said no, to come along. As the King will receive Bemis in the airport reception room, we can greet him informally as he leaves the plane and shove off without any appreciable delay in taking Bemis to the King. Stop frowning, sweetie. You'll have plenty of time to talk to Bemis tomorrow night."

"I was thinking about my camera. I suppose I daren't bring it if the King's in the neighborhood."

"I wouldn't."

"Oh, dear. Igor wanted a picture of the big American *Samoliot*. Will you pour your coffee, dear? Thank God, it's bubbling."

"Where are you going?"

"I must talk to Beryl's cook before he goes to Qam. Tomorrow is Marina's birthday. I want to give her a halva doll. The man in Marbhein said they sold bigger ones in Qam."

Ali Saif appeared. The palace again wished to speak to *Safir* Briscoe on the telephone. Thornton hurried to his study.

"Drench, again. Sorry to be such a nuisance."

"You're not, sir."

"About tomorrow night. I've just spoken to His Majesty. The King is most grateful for your invitation but he is certain both you and Mr. Bemis would prefer to dine *en famille*. So I suggested that His Majesty simply send his regrets through me."

"Whatever you think best, sir."

"Good. By the by, Rome has informed us that Mr. Bemis' flight is on schedule."

The Garden of the High Sun was, of course, designed for enjoyment at midday. In its center is a wide-basined fountain whose plumelike jets fall in curtains of mist and perceptibly cool the nearby air. Winding through hip-high mazes of flowers, paths radiate from the fountain, their marble pavements dappled by mats of shade from arching trees. Everywhere in the garden one can hear the plash of the fountain and, despite the immediacy of other flower odors, sense a pervading jasmine-like redolence. It comes from a thick growth of zambac, trellised hundreds of years ago to screen an ancient unused gate which once gave access to the stables. Now few know of the gate's existence.

When in residence in the Great Palace, Sajjid invariably repaired to the Garden of the High Sun for the third prayer. Today, while awaiting the summons from the minarets, he sat on the fountain's apron, listening to Uncle Wex's report on the successful experiments with the lignifying pear which had at last been made edible. Uncle Wex said he agreed with his assistants on its delicious taste.

"Let them be served at dinner, my uncle," instructed Sajjid. "Has an American flag been found?"

"It is already flying beside your own at the airport and Captain Firra'a reports that his musicians can now play the American anthem perfectly."

"My uncle?"

"Yes, my nephew?"

"I have a surprise for you!"

"You have?" Sajjid's eyes were sparkling. That meant that the King expected whatever he was about to say would be exciting. Well, please God, it would not be more Program responsibilities. There were enough now to keep one almost constantly in conference with officialdom, leaving precious little time for activities for which one was more fitted.

Sajjid closed his eyes in deep concentration on the strange language he was about to attempt to speak. "I am going to be doing what you are—no!—what you have advice me to be doing." Sajjid smiled at his error. "I study again the Engliss. Jolly good, is not?" Satisfaction with his verbal achievement glowed on Sajjid's face.

"Jolly good, indeed," agreed Drench.

Early in their friendship, Sajjid's father had been reluctant to admit anything foreign to Suruk other than Wexford and Lucy Drench. The argument of his persuasive sister, the Princess Budur, finally convinced him that he should have others about him who spoke English. As a result, bright Suruki students, now invaluable as co-ordinators with ASOCO and in diplomatic posts, were sent abroad to study. But in his boyhood, Sajjid had been taught no foreign language. Five years ago, when he had permitted geologists to examine the coastal region, he had been secretly embarrassed having to converse with them through interpreters. When ASOCO came into being, Sajjid had made one or two attempts to learn English with little success. Drench hoped the new teacher would achieve more than the American woman who, two years ago, had fled back to her classes in the oil company's school in Batrul Mina after eight discouraging weeks in which she had tried to make the King and his grown sons understand some of the peculiarities of English infinitives and tenses. Drench, himself, had long since abandoned efforts to make Sajjid realize that although spoken Arabic has no infinitive in the English sense, compared to the complexities of other Arabic verb forms, English conjugations were as simple as Esperanto. Also, Sajjid had never been able to relate properly nouns and prepositions. Thus, he could offer a listener only a headlong rush of confused speech, interspersed with Anglicisms Sajjid had heard Drench and his wife use when he was young. They were usually distorted when he employed them, but he seemed to know their meanings. Once, after an awesome display of the royal syntax, Beryl Hipp had confided to Drench, "His Majesty has more an awareness of English than an acquaintance." Drench could still remember Thornton Briscoe's first royal audience. Briscoe achieved diplomatic stature in Drench's estimation by never batting an eye under a cascade of such approximations as "six to one and half dozen another."

"In a month I do to be speaking maybe so good as Farha, by Jove."

"Good luck, my nephew." Sajjid's rekindled zeal indicated an intention to converse with Newton Bemis. Drench hoped the American would be able to make his way safely through this particular king's English.

The *muezzins* of the city began screeching the noonday call to prayer. As Sajjid prostrated himself toward Mecca, Drench bowed and walked briskly to the entrance of the palace. In the doorway he stopped. A butterfly had lighted on the door's outer grille. It was a *Vanessa atalanta,* a red admiral. So large a specimen was not common in Arabia. Drench moved to regard it more closely. He watched it dart toward the fountain. As it suddenly veered in its flight his eye was caught by the sun's reflection on an object behind the zambac. After a moment it was gone. Drench turned around and casually entered the palace.

The burlier of Ameen Abban's overnight guests, the one with thick cheeks and coarse lips, broke the silence behind the zambac. "The Englishman has gone."

"Be quiet!" whispered the one with the foxlike face. "I am timing the prayer. And stop glancing at your watch. When you lift your wrist the sun strikes the metal and it might be seen."

"I thought it had stopped. I don't think they gave us very good watches."

"Be silent. Mine is working." As Fox Face eyed the second hand's progress, he drank in the delicious scent of the zambac. Everything was progressing as he had been told it would.

You will leave the cart beside the old stables. The gate will be unlocked and oiled and will swing open easily. The Inglizi may also be there, but he will withdraw when the muezzins begin their call. The King always prays at least three full minutes. You will come from behind the shrubbery exactly one minute after he has begun.

Fat Cheeks toyed with the zipper on the large sack. With his free hand Fox Face halted him. "Keep it closed until we are behind him. It contains something that will make him sleep."

"It's heavier than most sacks."

"It is lined with rubber."

Fat Cheeks was about to ask if the sack's contents might not also affect him when he put it over the King's head, but the inquiry was frozen on his lips. A quiet but attention-calling cough had sounded behind them. Both men spun around. Wexford Drench, too, had found the gate unlocked and well oiled. The steadily pointed muzzle of the .455 Webley he was holding discouraged the intruders from taking advantage of his shortness of breath.

"Lift your arms and face the shrubbery."

Fox Face did so. Fat Cheeks tried to obey, but was slightly handicapped.

"Let the bag fall to the grass." Fat Cheeks complied. "If you want to stay alive you will stand quietly until His Majesty leaves the garden."

"We did not wish to disturb His Majesty," whispered Fox Face.

"Nor will you unless I have to shoot to keep you silent."

Until Sajjid rose to his feet and departed nothing was heard save the murmur of the fountain.

Drench then conducted the intruders to the palace's eastern gate. There the *askeri* guards disarmed them.

Jabil the Mat, free for an hour from his duties at the palace, strolled through the *suq*. As was his habit he stopped at the shop of Zarh, the shoe merchant, to exchange greetings. Today he tarried a bit longer than usual. After Jabil resumed his stroll Zarh surveyed the banks of footwear on display outside his shop. Apparently he did not like their arrangement. He shifted several pairs about, including two blue slippers at the end of the top row. These he replaced with a pair of red ones. When the churning stream of shoppers began to thin, a fifteen-year-old boy, his arms full of purchases made elsewhere, paused to inspect the rows of footwear. Zarh went to the rear of his shop. Noting the red shoes, the boy also went inside.

"You did not get the beets," complained Aysha, the cook. "I can not make borscht for Their Excellencies without beets."

"There was such a crowd in the Street of the Vegetables I was afraid I would be late with what you wanted for lunch. I'll get the beets this afternoon."

A buzzer drew the boy's attention to the room annunciator. The call was from the Ambassador's study. It buzzed again. "It is for me," said the boy, and he dashed from the kitchen. The cook's voice followed him. "If there is no borscht tonight it will be your fault."

The boy's name was Awadh and everyone in the embassy but Boris Voronsky considered him a bright but inconsequential houseboy. He entered Voronsky's study and closed the door behind him.

"There was a message?"

"Yes, Excellency. I was going to report as soon as I gave the cook my purchases."

"I assumed you had learned something," said Voronsky, "by the speed of your bicycle. Never race like that again. Such hurrying can arouse suspicion. What were you told?"

"Two men were arrested at the palace. They were about to seize the King while he was at his noon prayer. Jabil could not learn who they were."

"Do not name names. Refer to people as 'our palace friends' and so on."

"I shall obey, Excellency."

"Good. Did he see them?"

"No, Excellency. The *askeri* corporal told Ja—our palace friend they might be Lebanese; they spoke as though they lived in the north. One had an airtight sack."

"A sack? Why?"

"To drop over the King's head. It contained a drug to make His Majesty unconscious."

"Have the men been executed?"

"I don't know, Excellency. They were removed by the police."

"Have you something to justify going back to the city this afternoon?"

"Yes, Excellency. I purposely forgot to bring beets."

"Good. Thank you, Awadh."

The boy lingered in the doorway.

"You have more to report?"

"No, Excellency. I am seeing my mother tonight. She does not know about your kind promise. May I ask her consent regarding Moscow?"

"Is it quite necessary?"

"Oh, yes, Excellency. I am sure she will bless you for promising to send me to the Bolshoi School."

Voronsky weighed Awadh's request and decided it might be helpful if the boy's mother spread the news of his employer's benefaction. Awadh was indeed talented as a dancer and when the Voronsky-Boyschekov plan was realized, the scholarship would enhance local good will.

"Very well. But do not say the invitation came directly from me.

You must tell your mother it was my wife who discovered how talented you are and told you how eager Russia is to foster promising artists. Above all you must not mention the secret diplomatic training I have been giving you."

Awadh had not wept since he was twelve and he repressed the surge of gratitude that almost choked him. "May God be as good to you as He has been to me, Excellency," Awadh managed to say before he left the room.

Voronsky pondered. The plan he and Boyschekov had so carefully worked out might now have to be altered. The events of this morning called for a reappraisal of His Beneficence as a proper candidate to supplant Sajjid.

Now it was disturbingly clear what His Beneficence had meant by "developments you may soon learn about." The idiot! Employing a pair of clumsy cutthroats to perform an act that required delicacy and skill. It was inconceivable that Moscow continue negotiations with such a bungler. Boyschekov's inclusion among the scientists at the agronomy station could now more than justify itself. Should the Bureau insist on another protégé, any of several anti-Sajjid *sheikhs* in the north Boyschekov had been cultivating was available.

"They have identified your coffee house," said the *Nazir* of police, "as the place where they slept last night."

The *Nazir*'s eyes went to the traditional implements of torture which were being carted into the room. So did Ameen Abban's.

"You can avoid considerable pain if you tell me who paid you to shelter them."

"I will speak," said Ameen Abban.

He was told to wait. The room was cleared of everyone but the *Nazir* and Wexford Drench. The *Nazir* sighed with relief. Fortunately, this terrified culprit was unaware that torture was now officially prohibited. Deprived of thumbscrews and other devices, it would have been difficult to extract a confession with the King's tender-hearted friend present.

"Now," demanded the *Nazir*.

Drench and the *Nazir* reported the substance of the confessions. Inwardly shaken, King Sajjid maintained an outward calm. "I do not know a man named Jala Hisim."

"He is a clerk in the office of His Beneficence," said the *Nazir*.

"A confidential clerk," clarified Wexford Drench.

Sajjid stared. "It is fantastic. You are certain there has been no mistake?"

"Jala Hisim confessed he engaged them in Beirut, arranged their transportation to Qam and paid the coffee house owner to hide them."

Sajjid pondered. "It is very distressing. Is His Beneficence in the city?"

"He is waiting at the house of Hisim's brother in the village of Daia Akhdar. He expects Hisim and the two Lebanese to take Your Majesty there as soon as it is dark."

"You are certain he has not learned of the arrests?"

"He has had no opportunity, Greatness. Daia Akhdar is two miles beyond the airport. My men there saluted His Beneficence when his Cadillac went in that direction shortly before noon. That would have been about the time the Lebanese entered the palace grounds. No one has traveled the road to Daia Akhdar since then. What shall I do, Greatness?"

"Bring him to me."

"Wait, my nephew." The others looked at Drench. "Daia Akhdar is walled and has two gates. If the *Nazir* puts *askeris* at both they can detect anyone bringing news of the plot's failure. If His Beneficence tries to leave the village he can easily be prevented."

"My uncle, I bask in your wisdom." Sajjid turned to the *Nazir*. "If he tries to escape bring him to me immediately."

When the *Nazir* had gone Drench sought to lessen the torture he could see Sajjid was suffering. "Your love for the child he once was is blinding you to the evil in the man who has tried to kill you."

"It would have been better if you had let him."

"So you could then avoid the truth?"

"The truth is scalding."

"You must cool it with your reason. You have long known he did not merit your affection." Sajjid closed his eyes, but could not shut out the truth of what he was hearing.

"You are right, my uncle. I have been guilty of softness. If his plot had succeeded, Suruk would have suffered more than I. I shall no longer think of him as a son."

Chapter 8

Being an automatic self-awakener, Newton had instructed the steward not to call him. Now daylight was filtering through the darkened bedroom. Almost immediately after Newton pressed the call button, the steward appeared.

"Good morning, sir. Did you sleep well?"

"Yes, thanks." Why explain that the continuing operation of the amphetamine dosages had denied him all but brief, fitful periods of the sleep his body so badly needed?

"Are we approaching Rome?"

"Rome is an hour behind us." The steward pushed back the window screen which had been drawn to shut out the sunrise over the Atlantic. "It's a beautiful day, sir. Right now we are over the Cyclades. Naxos is below us."

Naxos! Newton looked down excitedly, and was startled. Stored in his memory with other juvenile conceptions was Naxos as it must have been when the world was young. This wasn't Ariadne's verdant Dia where she had fled with Theseus only to find herself left in the arms of Dionysus. It was merely a ragged scrap of crumpled parchment, floating on an inverted sky, bleached and worn by time, showing no trace of what it had once invited men to read. He turned from the window. He ordered breakfast and then wondered if he could eat it. Fatigue was beginning to take its toll. It would be deplorable if he had to meet his royal host drained of energy. Well, if there was any truth in the reputed Arabian solicitude for guests, King Sajjid would not keep him up late tonight. Within a few hours, the drug's effects would have worn away and he would be able to sleep.

How grateful he would be to feel rested and refreshed. He hoped Rowena had been right in assuring him that, being freed from the constant demands upon his time and strength, he would find relaxation. With his activities at home in perspective, he could see that he had experienced very little relaxation since becoming engaged. There had been periods of excitement, of course, but even at the moment Rowena had accepted him he had not been entirely free of concern. Simultaneously he had been filled with an awareness of the responsibilities marriage would entail. Since then he had intensified his work schedule in order to justify spending more time with Rowena. He must have tired himself more than he had realized.

An hour later he was still abnormally wakeful. Through a lounge window he identified the long reaches of Iraq desert below. Mrs. Haruba emerged from her bedroom and joined him. She had donned the long black *fustan* and headscarf, the street garb of upper-class Suruki females.

"When we arrive, you will find it hard to distinguish me from other women because this and a masking veil are still required if one is respectable." The steward announced they were approaching Suruk.

"Yes," said Mrs. Haruba, "there are the Mountains of God."

Less than a mile below lay the snowy heights of Suruk's northern frontier.

Two minutes later the mountain crests were behind them. The plane leveled off to half its six-mile elevation. Two rivers like the bent prongs of a compass wandered through the grassland at the mountains' feet.

"They are named for two Muslim saints. The Stream of Abraham is on the left and the Stream of Alexander on the right. There is always snow on the mountains so the rivers never become dry. They feed our chain of *kanats,* underground canals which go through the farmlands. Where you see Abraham turning east is our only wasteland."

"Doesn't the river go through it?"

"Yes, but nothing can be made to grow there. It is very properly called the Land Beyond the Gate."

"What gate?"

"The one through which Adam was driven. It is now the place of execution for criminals as they are unworthy of burial in Eden."

A moment later what looked like a cluster of dusty sugar cubes floated below them. "That," said Mrs. Haruba, "is Akhor, our most northern community. The district around it is known as the Oven. It is unbearably hot in the summer but it is the chief city among several sheikhdoms."

The landscape began forming a patchwork of pastel colors, greens, pinks, and checkerboards which soon became primaries darkened here and there by shadows of orchards and woods.

A navigation check with the Qam control tower altered slightly the plane's course. Newton blinked as the adjustment suddenly brought into view a coruscation of distant lights. A moment later the sun's reflection passed from what now looked like a cluster of varicolored beads.

"Those are the domes of the city's mosques," said Mrs. Haruba. "The one that seems to be sapphire blue is really turquoise. It's the largest in all Suruk."

The steward interrupted. "We will be landing in five minutes. Will you fasten your seat belts, please?" From her purse Mrs. Haruba produced the completing touch to her Suruki costume, the silken *yashmak* and its protective silver bars which curve from the bridge of the nose and snuggle over the cheeks like an inverted V.

"Aren't they uncomfortably heavy?"

"Oh, no. They weigh just enough to keep the veil from fluttering in a breeze." Mrs. Haruba clamped her seat belt and settled back in her chair. "And now as a respectable Suruki lady, my face will not be disclosed to any man until I am once again on this plane bound for America."

Mrs. Haruba's assumption was incorrect. Even before she entered Qam her veil was to be quite suddenly removed.

The promise of bandmaster Firra'a that "The Star Spangled Banner" would be correctly played was approximately fulfilled. Certainly the performance was not as ghastly as Drench had dreaded. One or two passages caused Thornton Briscoe to wince and Dolly to shut her eyes. Fortunately, the jolts to their aplomb were unnoticed. Everyone but Drench was behind them, and Drench's eyes were on Newton, halted halfway down the steps from the plane under admirable self-control and patriotically holding his hat over his heart. Despite its leisurely slowness the performance ended at last. Newton waited, bareheaded, for its Suruki counterpart. He was spared hearing the livelier strains of "Allah Destroy Those Scabrous Dog-Sons of Harlots Who Have Dared Challenge the Might of Holy Suruk." Drench had pointed out to the Master of Protocol that, as the King would not be present in person at the landing platform, there was no need to risk disconcerting the visitor by rendering what was virtually a musical battle-cry calling for wild, ear-splitting screams and instrumental notes in about equal parts.

Drench introduced himself and presented Newton to the Briscoes, correctly ignoring Mrs. Haruba who, though only a few feet behind Newton, was properly remote from any participation in the greetings. Newton accepted the invitation to dine with the Ambassador and his wife the following evening and promised to avail himself of the embassy's hospitality whenever he wished. The Briscoes then withdrew to their waiting car and left the airport.

Fifteen minutes earlier, in Daia Akhdar, Wexford Drench's foresight had paid off. A man from the office of His Beneficence arrived from Qam. As he was about to enter the Hisim house he was seized and gagged. Having manacled his wrists under his legs, so that he could not stand up, the *Nazir's* squad of *khaiyali* stood over him in silence, forbidden to communicate with him in any way. They watched the *Nazir* go inside the house and wondered if he was informing His Beneficence about the plot against the King. All the *khaiyali* knew was that two assassins in Qam had been seized at the palace and whisked away before anyone could learn their identity. Was this muted wretch their accomplice? Had there been a plan to kill His Beneficence as well as the King? It was all very puzzling and disturbing.

The *Nazir* was finding it disturbing, too. After all, His Beneficence was an exalted personage and having been forbidden to tell him why the King desired his presence, it was not easy to maintain the proper deference while following orders.

"Immediately?"

"Yes, Beneficent One."

"It is the King's command?"

"Yes, Beneficent One."

"When did he give you this command?"

"Less than an hour ago, Benefi—"

"He gave it to you *himself?*"

"Yes, Beneficent One."

Even when he was at ease, the hyperthyroid eyes of His Beneficence, Prince Musallim, projected abnormally; now they seemed about to pop out of his head. Something had gone wrong. Yet the *Nazir* apparently was unaware of anything unusual.

"How did you know I was here?"

"When His Majesty's messenger could not find you at your palace, I believe a clerk in your office said you might be here, visiting his sick father."

Good. The work of the two Lebanese had merely been delayed. Yet why was the *Nazir* being sent on a messenger's errand?

"Where is the King now?"

"At the airport. His Majesty is greeting his guest from America. But if you wish to wait for him at the Great Palace . . ."

"We will go to the airport." Musallim sighed with relief. Preoccupied with the business at hand he had completely forgotten yesterday's instructions to be in attendance. The King had merely sent for him to be part of the reception committee.

"As you wish, Beneficent One." One might as well take him there. His Majesty *had* said, *"Bring His Beneficence to me."*

The *Nazir's* men watched His Beneficence come from the house, followed by the *Nazir*. Both got into the *Nazir's* car and the *khaiyali* were ordered to form an escort before and behind it, as they would have done on any important occasion.

"His Majesty is here to welcome you himself," said Drench. "He is in the private reception room." The two men walked toward the main airport building between double rows of royal guards; Mrs. Haruba a few feet behind them.

"When will it be permissible for me to speak to Mrs. Haruba again?"

"Any time. Not in public I'm afraid. But whenever you want her services you may summon her to your office."

"My office?"

"A room has been fitted for your use. Here we are. This is the reception room. We can resume our talk at the palace, where I'll be happy to—" Drench stopped because of what he saw through the open door. His Beneficence, the visibly agitated *Nazir* by his side, was an animated conversation with the King. A little apart from the trio, Drench saw Sajjid's attendant dignitaries gazing blankly as their ruler and His Beneficence seemed to be trying to glare each other down. In his forty-five years residence in Suruk, Drench often had had to adjust himself to sudden interruptions of ceremonial procedures. (At his coronation, Sajjid had delayed the ceremony for half an hour because of the sudden desire to have six-year-old Jahuar fetched from the royal nursery to watch his father be crowned.) Drench did his best to minimize the present contretemps. First, he casually closed the reception room door and smiled at Newton.

"I'm frightfully sorry, but His Majesty cannot greet you immediately. I fancy the delay will be brief. Was your journey comfortable?"

Newton said it had been very pleasant. As if there were nothing else on earth worth talking about, Drench said he had never flown in any kind of plane and pressed Newton to tell him what it was like to fly in a jet.

"Does it shake you up a bit?"

"Not at all, sir."

"Fancy that. How high do you go?"

"It varies, sir. Usually between thirty and forty thousand feet."

"Fancy that. Now about the sounds the passengers hear. They're not too noisy, I'm told."

Newton patiently answered every question, occasionally glancing to where Mrs. Haruba stood motionless fifteen feet away. Apparently, by Suruki standards of decorum, even being within earshot of the two men would have been an impropriety.

In the reception room the puzzled members of the royal suite might just as well have been miles away.

"Why do we to be speak the Engliss?" asked His Beneficence.

"Because if those people being here do know what was you do, they do to kill you before I do command you die. I speaking Engliss so you not to be shooted before you confess. You now knowing?"

The *Nazir,* though uncomprehending, was prepared for possible violence. With his trigger finger on the revolver under the folds of his *thobe,* he saw the mouth of His Beneficence open wide in astonishment. With his voice at a conversational level, Sajjid continued.

"Why you go to telled those peoples to go and be killing papa of you?"

The baffled listeners heard something like an "Oh!" of astonishment from His Beneficence, followed, after a moment of indecision, by "*Wagid alaina!*" Why was Musallim saying it had been his duty? In the overall conversational darkness the words shed no light.

"Engliss! To be speaking the Engliss!" demanded Sajjid. Noting the defiance in the young man's eyes, the *Nazir,* for expediency, moved so close to Musallim that he could feel the muzzle of the *Nazir's* concealed gun touching his third rib.

"I do not telling those other people to go to killing you, papa."

"They have bag for to putting over head of me. With drugs inside to it for to killing me."

"Not for killing you. Only to making you—*nam*. What *nam* in the Engliss?"

"Sleep."

"To making you sleep. Then you are coming to Daia Akhdar and we to be speaking about why do you treated me so bad."

"I treated you much, much gooder as you do deserving."

"I do deserving to know why brothers of me now do having your favor, not me. Wherefore why you are to be brong to me is for to making peace. If you speaking, 'Yes, now I be good papa and not be denying what are your right to having,' you not dying and I ask blessing by you."

"You having no right of nothing."

"When Jahaur die, you say me are to be heir onto throne. It is be truth, yes?"

"No, not truth. I speak, 'Maybe, yes.' Never, 'Right-ho, yes, indeed!' I speak you most old among sons of me and if you be to proved top hole, fine man I *then* will speak, 'Right-ho.' You do speak, 'Yes, yes, papa. I do be fine man. I will going make *hajj* to Mecca.' I do think, 'Jolly good! Because he willing go to Mecca, three cheers. Maybe he having goodness inside.' I speak to Minister of Money, 'Give the son of me what many *dinar* he want.' And what do I finding out you do? You do not to make *hajj*. You do going to Beirut. You do going buy apartmental house for bad womans you finding in nightsclub. Do not be to look surprise. Do you thinking these Minister not telling to me how you spended money? I say, 'Yes, yes, quite right, by Jove. I tell him to buy.' I speak that because why? Because I not wanting peoples to knowing you not do going to Mecca. One day on telephone you speak, 'Hello, Papa. I do have made *hajj*. Now I do come to home from Mecca.' I command to find out where do you are speaking on telephone. I founded you say hello from Beirut. So I do know you telled lie. And wherefore I say to me, 'These son of me do not be honest and good man, and he never cannot be noble king!' Now you are knowing why I did to refusing private speaking with you since you do came back from not to making *hajj*."

Sajjid looked about him. Uncle Wex could not be expected to keep Mr. Bemis engaged much longer. Also, the increasing concern and perplexity on the faces of his attendants made it advisable to hasten the conclusion of the interview in Arabic.

"Gentlemen, I have had to discuss private matters with my son and now will all but the *Nazir* and General Barim join Professor Drench and apologize for my detention here. Professor Drench will present you to my guest, Mr. Bemis. I shall invite you back within a few minutes. Thank you."

Murmurs of deferential acquiescence wafted back until the room had cleared of all witnesses but General Barim, the head of national defense, and the *Nazir*.

Seeing a group of bearded dignitaries emerging from the reception room made Bemis think the conference was over and that he would now be presented to his host. One of the group spoke briefly to Drench. In return Drench seemed to be asking the man a question. In the *lingua franca* of gesture, the high shrug of the man's shoulders emphasized his being at a loss to reply. In Drench's next question Newton thought he heard the word "Inglisi?"

"*Aiwa, Ustaz*," said the official. Newton's fragmentary Arabic was sufficient to recognize the word for "yes" and the word for "professor" the Western diplomats had turned into "Eustace."

Drench turned to Newton. "His Majesty is still engaged, but he would like me to present the members of his Cabinet, who are also here to greet you." He indicated the group's spokesman. "This gentleman is Amir Ma'arouf al Zaman, His Majesty's Minister of Agriculture."

For the next few minutes, a succession of alternating ceremonious bows and muscular handshakes that made him wince handicapped Newton's earnest effort to memorize elaborate titles and lengthy names. Nevertheless he did his best.

Having recounted in Arabic to the *Nazir* and General Barim the substance of his talk with his son, Sajjid concluded: "And now, if he wishes to avoid public death, he will go with you quietly. Tonight we shall decide what his punishment is to be." He looked at his son, hopeful of some indication of contrition. There was anything but penitence in what Musallim offered as a parting shot.

"I did nothing as bad as you did to your own father." Sajjid stared. Had someone been circulating those old lies again?

"What foolishness have you been listening to?"

"Was he not poisoned?"

"Yes, because he ate what he had been told he should not eat."

"Were you not with him when he died?"

"I was. And so was his secretary. She, too, had warned him." The *Nazir* and General Barim had been as astonished as Sajjid at the young man's preposterous charges. Had he never bothered to learn the established facts of his grandfather's death?

"And she, too, is dead!"

General Barim exploded.

"Majesty! His Beneficence is insane!"

"No," said Sajjid sadly. "He is troubled with delusions. Why do you think she is dead, Musallim?"

"She is not here to support your story."

"General Barim, Mrs. Haruba has come with Mr. Bemis. Would you bring her to me?"

A military figure emerged from the building and went directly to Mrs. Haruba. She silently followed him into the reception room. Once again the door closed.

The welcoming smiles firmly riveted on the faces of the Cabinet members indicated total inattention to the incident. On the other hand, when Drench immediately resumed introductions, Newton felt that the recital of the many names of the Minister of Canals and Rivers was in a slightly slower tempo than that Drench had used in identifying the others. Had Drench been disconcerted by Mrs. Haruba's summons to the Royal presence? Was it customary in Suruk for its King to receive a guest's entourage before he welcomed the guest? Another bone-crushing handclasp emphasized the delight of another beaming excellency.

"You chose to believe the stupid gossip about Mrs. Haruba's absence. She has been in America. Had you asked, I would have told you. You see she is here. Mrs. Haruba, you will tell my son exactly how my father died."

A momentarily quavering voice grew firm and confident when the eyes above the veil saw that the King and his officials were watching only the face of the King's son.

"Because his late Majesty took great interest in the work of his plant experts, he had ordered that a *kuta,* the first result of a crossbreeding of tomatoes, be shown to him. When the *kuta* arrived, the botanist who brought it told me that while the crossed species were themselves quite harmless, their offspring might be poisonous. He explained that the tomato genus includes the plant called nightshade and that its dangerous alkaloids might have recurred in the experimental *kuta.* I was showing the specimen to His Greatness when His Majesty joined us.

"His Majesty observed that the skin and coloring of the *kuta* were those of the tomatoes he had been in the habit of eating. His Majesty cut it in half and said it looked appetizing. He would have tasted it had not His Greatness and I told him of the risk he would be taking. His Majesty laughed and said that at one time all tomatoes had been thought to contain alkaloids and this one could not possibly be harmful. We repeated the plant expert's warning and I started to move away with the plate when His Majesty snatched one of the cut halves. Before His Greatness and I could protest further, he had put it into his mouth. 'It is delicious and quite harmless,' he said. Two minutes later His Majesty was dead."

"Thank you," said Sajjid. "My son will now do what I have commanded him to do." Silent and crushed, the young man obediently left with his two escorts through the street door.

Twice within a few hours Sajjid had been shocked by harrowing incidents. One had hurt him cruelly as a father. The second was less painful but equally upsetting.

Did this foolish, vengeful woman believe he had not recognized her voice?

"May I retire, Your Majesty?"

"Not yet. You told the story very well."

"Because it is the truth, Greatness."

"Yes. But not a truth which you witnessed."

"Then how would I know it?"

"Because the woman you pretend to be told it to you. I wish to see your face, Aunt Budur."

Her trembling hands removed the veil. It was indeed the face of his father's sister. But a much older face than the one he had last seen blazing with grief and horror eight years ago. Then, like Sajjid's son, she too had believed Sajjid a patricide. The day of his father's funeral she had left Suruk. Sajjid had permitted her modest fortune to be turned over to an American bank, with the provision that she would never return. Yet here she was, defiant of his edict. Was it possible that Aunt Budur was contrite? If so, why had she not written him and asked forgiveness? Or was she still filled with hate? Aunt Budur of old had rarely allowed her opinions to be altered. Knowing Mrs. Haruba, she could have heard the truth about the fatal *kuta,* but remained adamant in her conviction of

Sajjid's guilt. Learning of Mrs. Haruba's assignment to accompany Mr. Bemis, she might have done away with the woman and taken her place. Aunt Budur would know that the likelihood of Mrs. Haruba's encountering Sajjid would be slight. Women in harems live on intrigue and Aunt Budur might have felt certain that even if some of the older women recognized her, they would not betray her presence. At the time several of them had resented her banishment.

"Where is Mrs. Haruba?"

"In the State of California. She was about to have a holiday, and knowing I was sick with hunger to see Suruk once more before I died, out of pity she timed her leave of absence that I might come in her place. She told me what her duties would be. I do not type very well, but I hoped to serve Mr. Bemis with reasonable efficiency and return with him to America as inconspicuously as I had arrived."

Sajjid's impassive silence disturbed the Lady Budur. It was possible that the years and flood of wealth had changed him from the strong-willed but forbearing youth to a vindictive despot. Disobedience to royal commands in the past had often brought death. Could it be that her nephew was now considering such retribution? Death would put an unpleasantly abrupt end to all she had planned to do, but it might be preferable to other retaliations wrathful rulers had exercised on their victims in Suruk's past.

"I have not decided what to do with you," said Sajjid. "Even if true, your confession does not lessen the gravity of your offense. Its truth I shall try to determine. Can you tell me the place where Mrs. Haruba can be found in California?"

"Of course. She is in the city of San Francisco, at the Hotel Fairmont."

"You will write it down and give it to me later." He rose. "You and my son have made me unforgivably rude to my guest from America. I do not wish him to be further discommoded. You will ride into Qam as Mr. Bemis would expect you to do. When he goes to his apartment, you will come to my office with Mrs. Haruba's address. When I am satisfied that she has come to no harm, I shall decide on the penalty for your disobedience. Replace your veil and tell Professor Drench I am at last able to welcome my guest."

Chapter 9

Of course, Newton rationalized, it wasn't really like a nightmare. In nightmares you wouldn't feel the heat; certainly not this much. And heat, brain-shriveling heat, was ever present in the jumble of experiences he was finding it so hard to coordinate. It required all his effort to stay awake. It had been hot enough standing hatless in the sun while that royal band made mincemeat of "The Star-Spangled Banner"; worse during the delay outdoors while pretending not to notice the discomfiture of Professor Drench at the King's preoccupation. There had been momentary relief in the comparatively cool reception room while Drench was presenting him to his host. In fact, he felt reasonably alert until the King opened his mouth. Had he really heard those double streams of sound; the King's stumbling, disjointed English phrases and Drench's simultaneous running efforts to clarify the royal distortions of syntax? It had actually happened, all right, because at the finish of his verbal confusion the King had flung out his arms like a man pleading for mercy and Drench had managed to explain that Sajjid was apologizing for having kept Newton waiting. Another assurance that he was not dreaming was the taste in his mouth. There must have been some thirst-quenching drinks among the bottles in those ice-filled buckets which had suddenly appeared in the reception room. If he hadn't been so vitiated he would have had the sense to ask what they were. He could still hear his host's enthusiastic approval when he had indicated one shaped somewhat like a Coca-Cola container: "Yes, yes, Misser Bemis! Those drink you do to chose are bang up top hole." Still, tasting the heavy sugar content of the portion he had got down had enabled him to fight invading drowsiness and accompany the King to his car. But the moment the car had started toward Qam the heat had again exerted its stupefying oppressiveness. Now another experience, undeniably factual, was clamoring for recognition by his consciousness.

"You are know who to be are all those peoples on horses, Misser Bemis? *Askeri* of me. Soldiers men. All guns do been shooted for say hello. Soldiers do raising Lord Harry to be like saying 'Happy welcome of Suruk, Misser Bemis!' "

The shrieking horsemen standing in their stirrups and the long-barreled antiquated guns being fired in the air were straight out of an almost forgotten Burton Holmes movie travelogue. But here the furious galloping back and forth was on a concrete roadway, so there weren't the great clouds of dust that had swirled about the riders in the picture, as they swept past some Arabian potentate being paid deafening homage on his birthday. Was it possible the great man in the travelogue had been Sajjid's father? The damned heat was becoming unbearable. He mustn't let it knock him out. What a coincidence if the man sitting beside him were in fact the son of . . . The gunfire and shouting were becoming less harsh, starting to blend into a soothing murmur. He closed his eyes to shut out the scorching glare. If the man beside him were . . .

Sajjid's voice made him open his eyes again. He was still sitting beside his host. The car had halted in a kind of courtyard. Thank God they were in the shade of a high wall which hid the sun from sight.

"All childs of peoples in palace. Also to be saying, 'Hello for Misser Bemis!' "

The whirling objects were children all right. There must be at least a hundred of them, none more than nine or ten years old. All were dancing, if you could call it that, to the shrill music of two fifes and what might be a kind of bagpipe. Its whine was low and screechy. Though discordant the instruments maintained a rhythm which was stressed by the vigorous hand-clapping of an audience of adults. Most of the little boys moved in tumbling, churning groups, forming and reforming circling patterns about single small figures who spun like tops in the centers of each vortex of dancers. As if on signal, a deafening shriek from the throats of onlookers and dancers brought the frenzied exhibition to a stop. The adults turned their grinning faces towards Sajjid's car as the children in one movement prostrated themselves on the courtyard stones.

"You are thought they to be good, Misser Bemis?"

"Very good, indeed, sir."

"Right ho!" Smiling, Sajjid turned to the silenced gathering and told them that the great man with him had enjoyed the *douidars'* performance. Immediately the children scrambled to their feet, laughing and chattering, many running to be hugged and kissed by admiring relatives.

"Now we to go into what are house of me. He now to be house of you as also."

Newton pried himself into wakefulness.

Sajjid had disregarded traditional royal decorum by personally accompanying his drowsy guest to his apartment. When Drench arrived with the servant carrying the great man's luggage, Sajjid asked Uncle Wex to familiarize Misser Bemis with the provisions for his comfort.

Above a wall telephone near the door was a printed card listing intra-palace telephones. One or two had check marks against them. The first, Drench explained, would connect Bemis directly with his apartment. The second would reach Mrs. Haruba. Newton said he would like her help in calling America. Drench, not yet informed of her unmasking, said: "Just call her room. She'll put Marbhein to work on it immediately."

The call to Mrs. Haruba was unanswered. Drench was certain he had seen her enter the palace from one of the cars in the King's motorcade. The palace operator assured him her telephone was working all right; it could be heard ringing. Rather than keep Newton waiting Drench, himself, telephoned the Marbhein exchange and instructed the manager to expedite Newton's overseas call.

"I'll dash along and see where Mrs. Haruba has taken herself. I'm sure she can't have gone far. If you have any difficulty with your call or want anything else for that matter don't hesitate to telephone my apartment. If I'm elsewhere, just dial the number I've marked: '*douidar.*' That'll fetch one of the pages, and if you merely say 'Drench,' he'll find me and deliver the message you give him."

Drench left.

Nuri dashed up the stairs to *Ustaz* Drench's quarters and delivered the note from the Chief Butler. He waited until the *Ustaz* finished reading.

"Did you see me dance, *Ustaz?*"

"Of course I did. I was in the car just behind His Majesty's. You were very good. Tell the Chief Butler I shall inform Mr. Bemis about the change in time."

"Should I find the man who winds the clocks?"

"Why?"

"They are resetting them?"

"This note has nothing to do with clocks. It says that dinner will be two hours later than the scheduled time. Mr. Bemis was very tired when he arrived from America and His Majesty wants him to enjoy a rest before we dine."

"How long will he stay, *Ustaz?*"

"I don't know and won't guess. And I intend to take a nap myself. Shoo!" The last word was new to Nuri's ears. It must be an English one, but the *Ustaz* was pointing emphatically to the door so Nuri did not ask for a translation.

Newton unpacked and looked about his chamber. It was a

big room with high ceilings, but its temperature was curiously pleasant. He soon saw why. The large grilled vents set just above the floor line in opposite walls were sending in currents of cool air. Had he looked up when he arrived in the courtyard, he told himself, he would undoubtedly have seen lofty wind towers high above the palace, ingenious devices by which Arabians for centuries had kept their dwellings comfortable in even the most scorching summer heat.

The telephone rang. In garbled English the Marbhein operator reported that connection had been made with the United States but that Washington had reported him that the person His Excellency had called was not in the place where was the telephone, but would *rentré* later in the day. The operator was at His Excellency's service, please. Newton asked that another call be made in a few hours. There was silence. The operator in Marbhein had disconnected.

On leaving, Drench had promised Newton he would be undisturbed until a half hour before dinner. O.K., when Drench wakened him he'd ask to have Marbhein make another try at six P.M., Washington time. What time was it there now? He looked at his own watch. Its hands indicated 11:10. Ten after eleven? Had he fallen asleep without even being aware of it? No, *now* he remembered; he had synchronized his watch with the pilot's just before they had reached Qam. Thick screens at the windows kept outside light from entering. He forced one open. Eleven-thirty and the sun was only now beginning to set! Well, whatever hour it might be elsewhere, it would not be dinnertime in the palace until it was quite dark. He had at least an hour, perhaps more, to rest. He was too tired to remove even his shoes. About to throw himself on the comfortable-looking bed, he saw objects on the table beside it.

Two cards were propped against a lamp. On the larger, under a royal monogram was embossed Arabic script. The smaller's typescript was in English:

TRANSLATION OF HIS MAJESTY'S STATEMENT TO MR. BEMIS: "I HOPE MR. NEWTON BEMIS WILL PLEASE ACCEPT THIS POOR TOKEN OF THE JOY I FEEL IN WELCOMING HIM TO MY COUNTRY.

SAJJID"

Beside the cards was a small gold box, its cover etched with the the same crest as the note. Newton lifted the lid and was jerked awake once more. Resting in the box was one of those extraordinary watches *Fortune* had described last year in an article on ultra elegant Christmas gifts; a platinum-cased *Parronde-Huissot,* small enough to be carried in a vest pocket, but with a mechanism comparable with that of one of the master chronometers in the Naval Observatory. Perhaps, the *Fortune* writer had speculated, because a luxurious yacht could be bought for about the same price, of the six *Parronde-Huissots* in existence, two had yet to find purchasers.

Newton tried to think. What kind of service could he possibly render that would warrant the bestowal of a rarity like this? Or was it just a gesture of hospitality consistent with Sajjid's previous demonstrations of lavishness? Perhaps this unbalanced Croesus felt that a guest from abroad should find something more than fresh flowers in his bedroom. The thought of accepting it was as sickening as that drink at the airport. Possibly Mrs. Haruba could advise how to return it diplomatically. She might be in her room now. He dialed her number. Again there was no response. Should he ask Drench? No, Drench would no doubt feel he should follow the King's wishes and, after arguments, insist on its retention. Where could Mrs. Haruba be? If she had been assigned to other duties could he seek secretarial help from the American Embassy? And if the Ambassador could spare someone would he or she be permitted to enter the palace? Maybe it was foolish even to anticipate the need of a secretary. When in the name of God would someone tell him what he was expected to do?

He stretched out on the bed. What a preposterous situation to be in. And what a fool he had been to be persuaded that his coming here might be useful. *"Being in personal contact with the King for even a day or two might be invaluable to us."* What could an inexperienced investigator learn from a monarch who insisted on speaking in almost incomprehensible English? And that damned watch. If he had to accept it, maybe presenting it to a museum would take away his neurotic stomach pains. He closed his eyes to shut out the surroundings of his predicament. Exhaustion took over and his mind closed shop.

Drench's telephone call wakened him. Newton reported truthfully that he felt quite refreshed and assured the professor that he had everything he needed for his comfort.

"Good. In half an hour I'll drop by and pick you up." Newton's watch told him he had slept for almost three hours. Perhaps he could get Mrs. Haruba's counsel now. He dialed her number and waited. He dialed again. Perhaps she had been told he was resting and had gone to her own dinner.

The enormous bathroom was completely modern. One could almost swim in the sunken marble tub. Relaxing his mind as well as his body, he recalled the lessons in Arabian etiquette he had received from Priest and Mrs. Haruba. They had said that when sitting on the floor it was rude to allow the soles of the feet to be seen. Another point both had mentioned was that in audiences with Sajjid it would be Newton who must end the interview, otherwise good manners could make it last indefinitely. Surely even in Qam the host would indicate when a meal had ended? He would ask about that when Drench came for him.

Chapter 10

Newton, sitting on Sajjid's right, understood most of what he heard between royal mouthfuls; Drench, on the King's left, now and then fielded what Newton couldn't catch. Newton's attempt to express proper appreciation of the *Parronde-Huissot* had been emphatically discouraged.

"Not so! Not so, Misser Bemis! Those watch not never so good as I do feel to have you to come to Suruk!"

Sitting cross-legged was proving not too uncomfortable because of the elevation provided by the pillow. Newton glanced at his fellow guests. In the great circle Newton thought he recognized half a dozen of the Cabinet members he had met in the afternoon. The three youths who had bowed so deeply on meeting him Sajjid had identified as "some of the sons of me." All their faces showed faintly of Sajjid's features but there were cranial variations. Different mothers, probably.

Once the meal had begun most of the diners were uninhibited in their enthusiastic enjoyment of the food prepared in honor of the King's guest. Had he not been informed Newton would not have guessed that what he was eating had arrived in boxes and cans yesterday from America. The palace cooks had tried to follow the accompanying instructions on how each item of food was to be served. Finding the results unsatisfactory the cooks had made the dishes more palatable. Newton wondered if the soup, as spicy as a fruitcake, had begun its existence as clam chowder. He had been told that only one Arabian dish would be served this evening and there was a moment of concern after he had scooped up a handful of what Drench assured him were creamed oysters. As he put them in his mouth he observed Sajjid looking at him eagerly, waiting for Newton's approval. Newton's smile of appreciation was prompted less by politeness than the happy discovery that two small objects among the oysters were grapes. With relief, he took a deep breath of the flower scents coming through the open windows on air no longer heavy with the afternoon's heat.

During one of the handwashing intervals a *douidar* approached, whispered a message to Drench and left the room. Drench spoke briefly with Sajjid in Arabic. Newton thought he heard both men distinctly say "Haruba."

"Please to excuse, Misser Bemis, Professor Drench say telephoning exchange is not to be able to making important collection."

"Connection," rectified Drench quietly.

"Jolly good, 'connection,'" said Sajjid.

"Was it about Mrs. Haruba's telephone?"

Sajjid looked at him sharply: "What do you say, Misser Bemis?"

"I thought that you might be talking about the telephone in her room. When I've called her she hasn't answered it."

"Oh, to fancy that! I . . . I . . ." Sajjid was plainly floundering. "What you think, Professor Drench?"

"I think His Majesty wants to say that the telephone call he referred to was not to Mrs. Haruba's room." There was an exchange of more Arabic. "His Majesty says he is going to assign you someone younger to replace Mrs. Haruba. He says you will find her very satisfactory."

Sajjid was again smiling in his direction. It would no doubt be futile to say he would much prefer Mrs. Haruba to any substitute. He remembered Mrs. Haruba had said she knew no shorthand. It might be Dr. Hunain had selected her largely because of her excellent English. Had her successor been chosen because of greater secretarial competence? What the hell did the King require of him that would necessitate replacing Mrs. Haruba? It was about time the mystery of his mission be clarified. Why should he tolerate further delay?

The King was relishing the novel taste of the Qam version of candied sweet potatoes. Newton stopped eating and considered the proper approach to the subject.

Sajjid gulped another bite and again smiled at him. "You wanting to ask of what to be eated next, Misser Bemis?"

"No, sir. I'm sure whatever it is will be delicious."

"Is ice creams. Some of kind you to knowing, but cooked in Qam. We having all flavors ice cream in Suruk. You do to like ice creams?"

"Very much. But I wonder if I might ask you a question, sir."

"A question? Please to do, Misser Bemis."

"I'm afraid I'm quite ignorant—" Newton halted until "ignorant" was made clear by Drench.

"Right ho! Please to going on more, Misser Bemis. And to excuse do I to have help by Professor Drench."

"I say I'm afraid I'm ignorant about why you have been so kind as to invite me here." Drench's translation was cut off.

"No, no. I know what is Misser Bemis speaking. Misser Bemis, you do like to know what I do hope you can to do for me, right-ho?"

"Yes, sir."

Sajjid pondered. "Right-ho. Maybe many, many helps you can to do, Misser Bemis. Tomorrow I will to tell you one most of all important." He needed Drench's help again.

"His Majesty doesn't wish to discuss tonight something that deeply concerns him," Drench smiled. "I can promise you the advice he wants won't be difficult for you to provide."

"One thing I can to tell you now," resumed Sajjid. "You seeing those persons in red dressings? They from Akhor. Very noble *sheikh* persons."

Akhor, Newton remembered, was near the district Mrs. Haruba

had called the Oven. With Drench now being allowed to aid more frequently, Newton learned that the men had come to serve as part of the King's escort on his annual visit to their districts. Tradition demanded that Sajjid receive all who came to him in a ceremonial tent. Within its comparatively cool antechamber, Sajjid's callers waited for admission to the royal presence. The inner room in which they were received was always swelteringly hot. Did Mr. Bemis know of a way by which the tent could be air conditioned? There was a very simple one, Newton replied. He would have factory technicians fly down from Milan, possibly tomorrow, with portable air conditioning units and neoprene for coating the tent fabric. Workmen among Sajjid's subjects could be taught to operate the cooling equipment before the King had to leave Qam.

To emphasize his thanks, Sajjid seized Newton's hands and pressed them against his heart. Sajjid whispered to Drench who, in turn, beckoned an attendant. After a few words from Drench the attendant left the room.

The new secretary, said Drench, would be waiting in Bemis' office after dinner, and he could send a cable to Milan tonight.

Questioning Sajjid further became impossible. The ice cream arrived and proved to be delicious. As it was being consumed, a murmuring began among the guests. Smiling, Sajjid arose. An inquiry from him received a clamorous response. Everyone's eyes went to the door through which all the food had been brought. Three grinning cooks appeared to receive shouts of approval for the feast they had prepared. When they went back to the kitchens, a parade of servants entered. Each carried a great brass tray on which rested an object about two feet high covered with cloth of red silk. The trays were placed before the diners. The coverings were simultaneously whisked away disclosing large hookahs. The servants uncoiled the stems twined about them and offered the individual mouthpieces to the guests.

Drench rose and came to Newton's side. It would be quite proper, he said, if he and Newton withdrew as the King was obliged to hear addresses by several of the guests which might be boring as well as incomprehensible to Newton. Newton got to his feet as did the King and the rest of the company. Sajjid again pressed Newton's hands to his heart. As if Newton had successfully completed a performance in the theater, hearty applause accompanied him to the door.

Outside the dining room, Newton faced Drench determinedly.

"I assume you're not permitted to discuss what I'm to hear tomorrow, sir, and I don't want to embarrass you. But surely you can tell me what induced the King to offer me a fantastic fee, charter a DC-8 to bring me, and on my arrival give me the most expensive watch in the world. It just happens that I know I'm not that important to anyone."

"Let me try to ease your mind," said Drench. "I presume you saw an article mentioning yourself in the American magazine *Short?*"

"I did," said Newton, grimly.

"I recently read the article in an Arabian edition and showed it to His Majesty. It made him most eager to meet you and, if you found it within your province, discuss with you his intention to bring to his people some of the wonders of modern science."

"I wouldn't have the faintest idea of what would be either useful or useless to them."

"His Majesty has a comprehensive overall plan for material and sociological development. It was more or less completed a year ago and while he still considers it fundamentally sound, he has given it considerable re-examination during the last six months. I think he would like to discuss some of its generalities with you."

It was grotesque. He had gone without sleep for two days, and been hauled four thousand miles away from his work and personal problems because a pathetically gullible Maecenas had convinced himself the rot in *Short* was true.

"Professor Drench, it's a little late for the King to learn this, but I am not the omniscient boy *Short* said I was. Expecting any guidance from me would be a complete waste of time. You are his friend and advisor. You must know Suruk's needs better than anyone. Why doesn't he turn the whole problem over to you?"

"I am woefully ignorant of things outside the world of the botanist. Only in my own field have foreign technical advances been introduced here."

"Why can't the King get all the technological guidance needed from UNESCO?"

"I think he wants to discuss that with you."

"Why with me? I have some familiarity with physics, but I'm no more a technologist than you are."

Drench smiled, sympathetically. "I know you think him foolishly impetuous in bringing you here. I admit he can at times be eccentric, but I promise you he is not a fool. And he is truly grateful that you left your work to come here."

Drench was patently finding it difficult to phrase something in his thoughts. "I'm certain you are qualified to advise him on one specific subject. Forgive me for being enigmatic but I know His Majesty wants to acquaint you with it, himself. If you will be patient for the time being, I can promise you that your mind will soon be at ease.

"Now, if you will come with me, you will meet the young lady taking over Mrs. Haruba's duties. She is a niece of the King and her name is Farha. She is soon to be married and as brides-to-be must not be seen, she will have to take your dictation from behind a *purdah* screen. Otherwise the poor child's head covering would make it difficult to read her notebook. And, by the by, you may think me unconscionably rude in not introducing you. Unhappily in Suruk the dignity of the male is of grave consequence and even though she is a princess, Farha is still unmarried and would not expect to be treated as your equal."

They had stopped before a room on the second landing. Drench knocked and opened the door slightly so that his voice could be heard inside.

"May we come in?"

"I am ready, Professor."

Newton followed Drench through the opened door. It might have been an office anywhere, except for the framed sheet of black silk near the desk, held upright by light wooden supports at its bottom, about ten inches above the floor. Its height and width were sufficient to conceal anyone standing or sitting behind it.

"Welcome home, Farha," said the professor. "I've been away myself and learned only yesterday that you were back again. Did you enjoy school this year?"

"Oh yes! It was the loveliest year of all. I learned to ski!" The soft voice was throbbing with excitement. "Have you ever done it?"

"Years ago when I was a youngster like you. Your uncle's guest is with me."

"How do you do, Mr. Bemis? Did I pronounce your name correctly?"

"Exactly right," said Newton. How far did the Suruki go in making women realize their inferiority?

"Do you have an attendant, Farha?" asked Drench.

"Yes, sir. The slave, Tagir."

"Oh, she is an old friend of mine. *Masalkhair, Tagir.*"

"*Yis'id masak, Ustaz.*"

Drench had exchanged greetings with a veiled figure, huddled like a bundle in a corner of the room. Apparently even wardens were required when brides-to-be were in the presence of men.

"When you're finished with Farha," said Drench, "you can get a good night's sleep. Tagir will guide you to your apartment."

After an exchange of good nights, Drench left Newton to his work.

"Whenever you are ready, Mr. Bemis."

"Can you take shorthand?"

"No, sir, but if you dictate slowly I can write down what you say. Will you want copies? I can make them on Professor Drench's typewriter."

The telephone on the desk rang. It was close to where the girl was sitting.

‡ 121 ‡

"Would you answer it, please?" Newton watched a small hand lift the receiver and take it out of sight.

"It is the exchange in Marbhein. They have a message from America."

"Please ask what it is."

She was apparently writing it down. Now and then he heard what sounded like "Miss Maggravee."

"*Audanak!*" He knew that meant "good-bye." The small hand replaced the receiver on its cradle. There was a pause.

"Can you tell me the message?"

"Forgive me, I am looking at my notes. You wanted to speak to a Miss M-c-g-r-a-v-e-y?"

"McGravey. That's right."

"Good. I was not certain of her name. Miss McGravey left a message at her home which was telephoned to the Marbhein office. She said she was with an architect whose name you knew and that you will be very happy with the plans of a house he is designing for you."

Newton mastered his surprise. Misunderstanding his silence, the girl said she would be happy to read the text of the message again. Newton bade her do so and listened attentively until she finished repeating it.

"May I congratulate you, Mr. Bemis?"

How could Rowena have done such a thing? Hadn't he made his attitude on the house crystal clear? The girl behind the screen had asked something.

"What did you say?"

"I said I hoped you would accept my congratulations."

"About what?"

"About the house Miss McGravey says will please you. Miss McGravey is your secretary?"

"She is my fiancée." *What the hell was wrong with his power of communication? This was the third or fourth time he had failed to make Rowena understand something of importance. Why had he failed to make her see how he felt about those major changes to the*

Elkins place? If he had been more explicit in his objection, they wouldn't be committed to building the four-room garçonnière. *It would be years before they needed a guest house that big. And that goddamned new garage. Why hadn't he told her clearly that its small cost was irrelevant; that its construction would destroy a beautiful eighteenth-century stable, roomy enough to house several more cars than the Elkins had had? One thing was obvious, he must learn to be less subject to Rowena's enthusiasms.*

"May I wish you great happiness?"

The girl's voice penetrated his introspection.

"I beg your pardon?"

"I asked if might I wish you happiness." What was she talking about? There was a pause. "Because you are going to be married."

"Oh! Thank you. Thank you, very much." He was forgetting common decencies. The girl had generously disregarded his rudeness, and deserved more than curt answers.

"I've been told you are engaged, too."

"Yes, sir. Next week on the third day of *Shawwan* I shall be married here in the palace. I am sure my uncle would be pleased if you honored him by coming."

"Thank you. I met many of his friends today. Could your fiancé have been among them?"

"No, sir. He arrives tomorrow. He is the *Sheikh* Abdel Sadek. He lives in Akhor. It is in the north. Have you been there?"

"No. I came to Qam today, directly from the United States. Have you been in America?"

"No, sir. I have a dear friend who lives in the State of Kentucky. Do you live near Kentucky?"

"My home is in Vermont. You have a very young voice. Would I be rude if I asked how old you were?"

Farha was touched by the gentleness of his question. She had met several American men, but none who had been as courteous as this gentleman. His voice sounded young, too. Dare she ask him his age? No, it would be presumptuous. She was here to offer secretarial assistance, not social conversation.

"I am nineteen. Do you wish me to send some cables, Mr. Bemis?"

Why not? What would be gained by bedeviling himself with his personal concerns. He decided to send the instructions for the air conditioning of Sajjid's tent to New York. It would be only a matter of minutes before the Milan plant was alerted to action.

The girl had surprisingly little difficulty with the technical words. She read the cable back.

"Shall I send it immediately?"

"Yes, please. —No!"

He might as well end Rowena's misunderstanding. "I'd like to send one to Miss McGravey, too." He worded it carefully. "*Not accepting fee we discussed. Therefore Fannestock must be told we are not commissioning him. Sorry, darling, that my unwillingness was not made clear to you.*"

The girl reported Marhbein's assurance that the cables would be dispatched immediately, and asked what else she could do for Mr. Bemis.

"You might ask the palace operator if Mrs. Haruba is in her room."

"Mrs. Haruba?"

"Yes. She is from the Washington embassy and came over with me on the plane. I was told I could call her directly from my room, but up to now I haven't been able to reach her."

"You remember the number of her telephone?"

"It was seven."

The girl's inquiry of the palace operator was interrupted by the voice of the slave chaperone; when she stopped, there was a momentary silence behind the screen. Once more the small hand replaced the telephone on its cradle, slowly, its owner evidently preoccupied.

"It is odd. Tagir says that although she did not see it happen, the woman who came with you left the palace with a captain of the police soon after you had arrived and has not been seen in the women's quarter of the palace."

‡ 124 ‡

"Tagir doesn't know where she went?"

"No, sir. Shall I try to find out?"

What would it serve? The King's decision had been definite.

"If you will ask Tagir to show me to my rooms, we'll call it an evening."

At the girl's instructions, Tagir arose from her corner and went to the door and opened it. A current of air crossed the room bringing with it unfamiliar flower odors. Mrs. Haruba had said that after tonight the Gardens of Beautiful Deceit would not be at their best.

"Do you suppose I could see the *Janayin Billail* this evening before I go to bed?"

"Of course! I am sure my uncle would want you to see them. Tomorrow night they will have started to fade. As soon as Tagir sets my veil we will come with you."

Tagir returned to her corner and picked up a cylindrical object Newton had seen dimly beside her. She took it behind the screen and after a moment the two figures emerged. Tagir, though tall in stature, seemed short beside the girl, as the headdress was at least two feet in height. It rested on her shoulders like an inverted laundry hamper and was covered by a lacy mesh with narrow slits through which its wearer could view her surroundings. A curtain of alternating pink and blue ribbons dripped down its sides to handicap her vision even more.

The message from Drench caused the King to excuse himself from his guests in the dining hall. The professor was waiting in Sajjid's study.

"I finally got through and have talked with both Dr. Hunain and Mrs. Haruba. Mrs. Haruba is in California and confirmed the truth of everything the Princess Budur told you. She justified deceiving you on the grounds that while your aunt had long since truly regretted her misunderstanding of the manner of your father's death, she was convinced you would never forgive her.

"Dr. Hunain was distressed to learn about the deception practised upon you and is awaiting Your Majesty's instruction to discharge Mrs. Haruba from her post." Drench waited as Sajjid considered this information.

"My heart is lighter. Tomorrow we will tell Dr. Hunain that because Mrs. Haruba has so freely confessed her complicity and because of her compassion for my aunt, she may continue in service."

"And the Princess?"

"She is a stupid woman, but she has also admitted her error. I am inclined to be tolerant."

"Shall I tell the *Nazir* to release her?"

"The *Nazir* is not in Qam. Speak to Captain Zhibin; she is in his charge. Tell him she may return to the palace, but must avoid meeting Mr. Bemis—he might ask embarrassing questions. You have not asked about the punishment I have ordered for my former son?"

"I thought, my nephew, you might not yet have decided."

"I have. The *Nazir* and General Barim have taken him to the Land Beyond the Gate."

Chapter 11

"Originally there were three *Janayin Billail*," said Farha. "This is the fourth, and it was created in your sixteenth century. If you sit here, you will see it best." There was plenty of room on the long stone bench. Realizing the girl had no intention of joining him, Newton sat down alone.

It was a startling spectacle in miniature. Newton found himself looking at the backs of an army of Muslim soldiers, standing in ghostly silence as if waiting for the command to attack a crenellated fortress in the distance, which by a clever arrangement of perspective seemed half a mile away.

"You are seeing the walled city of Rhodes," said Farha. "In 1522 Suleiman the Great captured it after a long siege. It had been defended by less than three thousand Christian knights. When Suleiman learned that so small a force had withstood nearly one hundred thousand of his own warriors, his admiration for his vanquished foe was so great that he permitted all the survivors to return to Europe in their own ships. And if you were in Rhodes tonight, you could see in reality what is in front of your eyes. Does that puzzle you?"

"I'm afraid it does."

The headdress moved slightly. Newton heard its wearer laughing gently at his bewilderment.

"Have you not noticed a similarity in the height and shape of the flower soldiers?"

"Yes."

"That is because they do not represent human bodies. They are the gravestones one can still see in the cemetery Suleiman prepared for his own dead."

"But they seem to have heads."

"Those are the stone turbans customary on Muslim graves. If the moon were full it would be more evident that they are meant to be carvings."

There was the sound of other voices. Newton turned and saw shadowy figures at the garden's entrance. Farha's voice indicated annoyance.

"They are women from the harem also come to see the cemetery."

"Maybe we'd better visit the other gardens?"

"If you wish." Tagir preceded them to a grilled gate opposite the one they had entered. The gate gave onto an arbor through whose leafy roof flecks of moonlight made its path barely visible.

"I must tell you something about the other gardens," said Farha. "They are much older than the one we have just seen and represent the elements. They were begun even before the days of Mohammed, but not completed until Suruk had become part of Islam. The one we are about to see is the Garden of Earth and Air. The illumination here in the arbor is intentionally faint, so that what lies around the bend will be disclosed with sudden vividness."

It was. The perspective offered by the ghostly army and walled city had nothing like the artificial expanse realized by the designers of the Garden of Earth and Air. It revealed a vista comparable to the one that stretched to infinity on the highway across California's Panamints, which had stopped Newton's breath when he first beheld it. The seemingly vast plain before him now was carpeted with flowers which diminished to microscopic dots as they approached the distant foothills of the mountain range over which Newton's plane had passed. Like the real Mountains of God, their crests wore mantles of snow which glistened in the moonlight, and the eye was easily persuaded to believe that the lofty peaks were close to the real stars in the milky sky above.

The garden's silence was broken by Tagir. "*Indama kunti sagheerah sa'alti al-boustani kaif wada'a an-nujouma hounak.*"

Farha laughed. "Tagir says I once thought the gardeners had put the stars there too."

On the plane Mrs. Haruba had cited a Suruki saying that the native dialect could best be learned from camels. The guttural harshness of Tagir's speech seemed completely absent from the girl's. When Farha had spoken over the telephone, Newton had noted a soft, liquid quality. Now, as she replied to the slave's comment, her voice sounded like a harp being played with shimmering lightness. He closed his eyes the better to enjoy the music. He opened them as the voices of the other visitors indicated their approach.

"It is very rude of them," said Farha. "They should have waited until we left."

She spoke again to the slave, who hurried to the arbor entrance. "Tagir will ask them not to disturb us again until our tour is finished. We can go out this way."

She led him into an open corridor of flowering hibiscus.

"The next is the *Jnaini Moi,* the Garden of Water. When I was four the nurse who brought me said I could get wet and might even drown if I stepped beyond where she told me to stand. When you see it you will know why I was frightened."

The illusion they suddenly came upon was certainly convincing. More than a thousand years ago some genius had selected the theme of ocean waves crashing on a beach and created a series of great combers approaching the shore; one, seemingly about to engulf beholders, was at least twenty feet high, the curving foam of its crest halted the moment before impact. To the right and left other breakers could be seen gathering to crash. The green of the water and the white spittle of froth on the sand at Newton's feet had all been achieved by flowers, frozen in their movement by a magician's wand.

Neither Newton nor Farha had been aware that the slave had not rejoined them until her voice made them turn to the hibiscus corridor.

"*Tafaddal ya, Amira!*"

The slave's excitement communicated itself to Farha.

"Mr. Bemis, I must speak with someone. Forgive me!" She turned and rushed toward Tagir before her apology was completed.

If you don't speak the language, Newton decided, it's not eavesdropping to listen. Though they were out of sight just beyond the corridor's entrance, the moon threw the silhouettes of several figures on the sand of the make-believe beach. Newton watched the shadow of Tagir remove the girl's headdress. There were ejaculations by an older female voice and Farha's shadow became one with that of a third figure as she was embraced. In a moment they were again separate shadows. Newton gave up trying to distinguish voices when a fourth was added to the medley.

It was so unexpected Farha could hardly conceal her joy.

"Do I look at all as you remember me, Grandmother?" The Princess Budur turned to her old friend, the Lady Khadya.

"When she was ten, she had the face and body of a monkey and if I were not sure you and Tagir would contradict me, I would say that this could not possibly be Farha. How could a monkey become so beautiful? Do you remember me at all?"

"Of course. You were always beautiful to me, Grandmother."

"And now I am beginning to turn into an ape." The Princess silenced the chorus of protests.

"When did you arrive, Grandmother?"

"Today. Did you think I would stay away when I learned you were to be married?"

"But I thought Uncle Sajjid had forbidden your return?"

"As you see, I am here. The Lady Khadya says your mother is visiting Abdul Sadek's family."

"She returns tomorrow. Did she know you were coming?"

"No. I wished my visit to be unexpected."

To Newton the tempo of the meaningless conversation seemed to grow faster, accented by exclamations implying surprise or disbelief, sometimes followed by flurries of laughter. After a bit the shadows on the sand outlined the headdress being replaced. More scraps of talk, presumably farewells, died away. Tagir and Farha returned.

"Forgive me, Mr. Bemis. It was a relative I have not seen for a long time."

"If you would like to be with her, Tagir can take me to the last garden and then show me the way to my rooms."

"That would be discourteous to my uncle's guest." The protest was made with dutiful earnestness, but Newton sensed it was not heartfelt.

"What if I told you I would be pleased to have you run and catch up with your relative?"

"I would not be rude?"

"Of course not."

A happy sigh came through the lace and ribbons.

"Thank you, Mr. Bemis." She spoke to the slave. "*Khouzi addaif ila janayen an-thoumma ila janaheh.*"

"*Amtuki, ya mawlati.*"

"You are very generous to me, Mister Bemis. Tagir will take you to your apartment. Good night."

The small figure with its bizarre headdress moved toward the hibiscus corridor. The girl lifted her long skirts in order to run. Just before she dashed out of sight Newton glimpsed slender ankles and small, slippered feet. In a pigeonhole of his memory something clamored for recognition, but was gone before it could be identified. Tagir moved into the range of his vision and indicated the direction to the Garden of Fire.

In moonlight most red flowers lose their color. Newton blinked at the realism of those which seemed to spring from a fissure in the earth as tongues of yellow, green and scarlet flames. It took a moment's study to see that they danced convincingly because spasmodic puffs of air piped from the wind towers kept them in constant agitation. A few yards away the ripened sides of peaches offered rigid but charming reflections of the flames.

A cloud began drifting across the moon. His nod to Tagir was enough to make her turn and lead him back to his rooms.

The moment his head touched the pillow, distant sounds from the festive city became a lullaby.

Chapter 12

In Suruk when the King as chief magistrate considers appeals from lower courts the Sitting is called *al araf* (literally, the region between Paradise and *Janiannam*) because the appellants are in a purgatory of uncertainty. As was customary during *Ramadan* the Sitting began within an hour after the Moment of the Threads. On rising, Sajjid hoped his duties this morning would not detain him long. Today his conferences with Mr. Bemis would begin. Not the least important subject he would bring up would be the undertaking for which Uncle Wex had doubted Mr. Bemis' qualifications. At breakfast he refreshed his mind by reading *The Fountaineer*, the complexities of which Uncle Wex had attempted to put into Arabic. With renewed confidence he had replaced both the translation and the original book with its illustrations in a secret drawer in his bedroom. This morning's agenda did not threaten to be unduly demanding. Sajjid commanded the first case to be presented.

The supervisor of canals in the district of Yir sought punishment for a contractor for his delay in delivering covers for the surface openings of a score of *kanats*, which had become blocked with dust and sand carried into them by the wind of a sudden *khamseen*. Sajjid found the contractor guilty and ordered that he pay for the repairs to the *kanats* and, after delivering the covers, spend three months in jail. The *kanat* system was too important to the country's well-being to warrant leniency. Next, Sajjid heard the appeal of a thief. In Suruk sentences for the first and second offenses by thieves are imposed by *cadis* and call for fines, imprisonments, or both. For a third conviction a *cadi* again decrees the punishment, but as it is arbitrarily the severance of the thief's right hand, the condemned man may beg clemency of the King. Sometimes the sentence is made less severe. The man before Sajjid today had three times stolen *mihrabs*, the tiles set in niches of street walls indicating the direction of Mecca. Three times he had been arrested while trying to sell them to foreign souvenir hunters in the oil ports. Sajjid felt obliged to sustain the sentence of amputation. Sajjid felt happier denying the plea of an influential Qamini. In Qam, doors thickly studded with silver and brass are proud possessions. The street entrance to the plaintiff's house had one so massive visitors came from the country to admire it. Near the door was another feature often seen in front of Arabian houses, a stone "resting block" on whose flat top those carrying heavy loads can lower their burdens for brief respites to strained shoulders and backs. The householder charged that the block was being denied to its customary users and the appearance of his house impaired by the daylong usurpation of the resting stone by a scabious beggar, a former slave of the householder. It is a mark of grace to give a slave his freedom when one makes a *hajj*. The householder testified that on his own *hajj* he had piously freed the squatter. The ex-slave's nonappearance in court, he argued, proved the man's awareness that his appeal had no merit. In studying the court's agenda before the Sitting began, the official court aide had made inquiries of the householder's neighbors. He testified the reason the ex-slave was not present was because he was too feeble to appear and had been freed only after he had become old, blind, and pathetically crippled in a lifetime of service to his liberator. Sajjid commanded the wicked householder to expiate his offense against God and man by providing liberally for the beggar and forfeiting one-tenth of all his assets to the Program's proposed school for the blind.

After reversing a *cadi's* ruling on a final case, Sajjid withdrew to his study.

When Habibi wakened her, Farha's interest in her parakeet was automatic. Mechanically she poured the tangerine juice into her palm and crumbled Habibi's bun without the usual accompanying endearments. The long talk with Grandmother after Anissa and the other *harimi* had left the roof was so dismaying she had cried herself to sleep. Grandmother's words again returned to distress her. It was hateful to believe that Mama had deliberately deceived her. Since her nursery days Farha had been aware of Grandmother and Mama's dislike for each other. They used to quarrel frequently and the clashes of strong wills between the two beings she loved most had mystified and frightened her. Grandmother might still be inclined to disagree with Mama's decisions, but surely she would not insist that Abdel Sadek was an evil man and unfit to be Farha's husband unless she knew it to be true. Mama had said that the marriage agreement contained a proviso that Sadek would marry no more wives after Farha became his bride. Grandmother said it had been easy for him to make such a promise because Farha would be his fourth and by Islamic law he was prohibited from acquiring more. It was true that Mama had allowed Farha to believe Sadek was a bachelor. And Grandmother admitted the possibility that Uncle Sajjid had enjoined Mama for political reasons to disclose nothing about Sadek which Farha might consider objectionable. How could the dark cloud on her future be lifted? Having so narrowly escaped Uncle Sajjid's wrath, Grandmother herself dared not risk provoking it again by urging him to repeal the marriage contract. Grandmother was certain that unless Farha appealed to him directly he would give no consideration to her plight. But Farha was not sure of her own present status in Uncle Sajjid's affections. Of course, it was only affection that made her a niece; congenitally, she was Sajjid's cousin. But their attachment had always been close before she had gone away to school. Once he had said he wished she were a boy because all his sons except Musallim and the baby Jahaur were disappointments to him. Now even Musallim, who had been named the Beneficent One because of the grace he had found in Uncle Sajjid's eyes, was said no longer to enjoy his father's favor. She had not seen Uncle Sajjid since her return. He had decreed a Period of Lament following Jahaur's death and halted all operations to modernize Suruk. Was he still sad and embittered? Even if he was now reconciled to Jahaur's loss and willing to listen to her arguments, might he not be so engrossed in conferences and entertainment for Mr. Bemis that he would permit no intrusion of family matters? What would happen if she told Uncle Sajjid of her misery in a letter? Would he even read it before it was too late?

She bade the person scratching on her door to enter. It was Nuri with a sealed note. The apprehension with which she opened it disappeared as she read the miraculous realization of her hope. Uncle Sajjid had summoned her to his study! Nuri had been surprised to discover the Lady Farha in tears. Even more unexpectedly he was finding himself being hugged as though he had learned another song. Dare he tell her of the lifelessness of the wooden bird in the clock? Before he could decide, the Lady Farha ordered him to summon Tagir to help her dress, then speed to His Majesty's study with the reply that she would come immediately. When Tagir arrived a minute later, Farha was already under the *purdah* headdress.

Thin knives of sunlight had pierced the gaps in his bedroom curtains and pricked Newton back to consciousness. The embarrassing *Parronde-Huissot* confirmed his wristwatch's statement that he had slept nine hours, his longest sleep in years. He sprang from bed and rang Drench's room.

"Good morning, Mr. Bemis."

"Good morning, Professor. Did I wake you?"

"I get up with the sun. How did you sleep?"

"Like a five-year-old."

"What would you like for breakfast?"

"Is a soft-boiled egg obtainable?"

"Of course. Would you like tea? Or coffee, perhaps? Arabian breakfast coffee is a bit syrupy, but the chief cook tells me he has several powdered kinds; American brands you can choose from."

"Any of them will be fine."

"I'll also tell them to bring you some of our Suruki fruits that I am sure you have never tasted before. And by the by, there are two cables from America. I'll have them send them up to you immediately."

"Thank you. And can you tell me, Professor, when I might have my audience with the King?"

"Any time you wish."

"I'll be ready as soon as I've eaten."

"Then shall we say in an hour's time?"

"Right."

His breakfast arrived before Bemis was out of the tub. He discovered a tray so loaded with provender that it must have challenged the strength of the servant who had carried it from the kitchen. There were four bowls of different fruit, all unfamiliar. Several baskets heaped with every kind of *petits pains,* enough for a dozen people. Behind an array of pots of jams, jellies, marmalade, and honey were jars of every brand of American instant coffee. Uncertainty about how Newton liked to drink it had prompted someone to add to the conventional provision of knives, forks, and spoons, several paper straws for sipping. Incongruously a single egg nestled in a silver cup.

His eyes finally lit on the two cablegrams tucked among a cluster of hot-water pots. The first was an acknowledgment of his instructions to the New York office regarding King Sajjid's tent with the assurance that they would be followed. The second was shorter:

DONT BE FOOLISH DARLING WEBSTER SAYS REJECTING YOU
KNOW WHAT COULD BE UNPARDONABLY INSULTING EN-

DANGERING ENTENTE CORDIALE STOP HOUSE WILL BE UT-
TERLY BEAUTIFUL AND A JOY TO BOTH OF US STOP I LOVE
YOU

                                    ROWENA

Newton read the cable a second time. Leaving the lavish breakfast untouched he went to the telephone and again called Drench.

"His Majesty will be pleased that you came so quickly," said Mr.
Selim, Uncle Sajjid's clerk of appointments, "You may go to his
study."

Uncle Sajjid invited Farha to remove her burdensome headdress
in the kindest of voices.

"You are even more beautiful than your mother said you were."

"Thank you, Uncle Sajjid." Had Grandmother braved his anger
and achieved this audience?

"Were you wondering why I wished to see you?" He was smiling. Was that a good omen?

"Yes, Uncle Sajjid."

"I wish to know something about your school in Lausanne. Who
was the woman from whom you learned English?"

The question was confusing.

"I had my first lessons from Aunt Lucy Drench when I was six."

"Yes, yes. But who at Lausanne taught English?"

"There were two persons. Miss Harmes-Fenton taught the
smaller children and Miss Anderson taught the more advanced
classes." What was in Uncle Sajjid's mind that caused him to look
at the calendar on his desk then thoughtfully tap his fingertips?

"They are both skillful and patient?"

"Yes, Uncle Sajjid."

"Who is the principal of your school?" He had said *moudira*
which is female.

"It is not a *moudira,* but a *moudire.* His name is Doctor Lamacq."

"Will you send him a message for me?"

"Of course, Uncle Sajjid."

"I wish to employ either or both of these ladies. I have discovered my own English is not what I want it to be. I shall try to persuade Dr. Lamacq to give them leave of absence of two, perhaps three months. Why have you opened your eyes so wide? If I paid them ten times what they receive from Dr. Lamacq and give him a proper gratuity do you think he would refuse?"

"I wondered why you need fetch instructors from such a distance?"

"It is really none of your concern, my dear niece, but I shall tell you. I have found the teachers in the oil company school in Batrul Mina unsatisfactory. Professor Drench says your English is excellent. I desire instruction from the persons who helped make it so. I would gladly become your pupil if you were not leaving the palace so soon." As he spoke he wrote a reminder to the court calligrapher to send Mr. Bemis one of the scrolled invitations to Farha's wedding which went to all noble guests.

The sound of a convulsive sob stopped his writing.

"Why are you crying, my niece? Aren't you happy that next week you will be the wife of a great *sheikh?*"

Something of her grandmother's spirit fired her tongue.

"No! I have learned he is an abominable man!"

"He is *what?*"

"An abominable man, and cruel, and he is not thirty-two years old but fifty-two! And I think I would rather be dead than be made his wife!"

The blazing eyes were those of a Farha Sajjid had never seen, and in her voice he recognized something else—agonizing pain.

"Farha!"

His sharp tone stung like a slap and checked her sobs, which was all he intended it to do.

"My niece, you have been misled by the cackling geese in the harem. Those with marriageable daughters are envious of you."

"Can you, my uncle, say Abdel Sadek is a good man?"

"Be patient, my Farha, and listen to me. Because I love you I will tell you something that only your mother knows, and which

I forbade her to discuss. I have told Abdel Sadek you are close to my heart and said that if he made you unhappy he would have me as an enemy. He also knows that as my nephew by marriage he would stand high in my esteem. I have had no reason to think of him as a cruel man. Moreover, Farha, I have found him completely worthy of the trust I have put in him. It is not a thing that should concern you, but I will tell you something I did not even disclose to your mother when I gave my approval to the marriage contract. I tell it to my Farha because I believe I can rely on her silence. Abdel Sadek is the strongest and most influential man among all the northern sheikhdoms. He has pretended to be favorably considering the offer of two or three of the regional *ashraf* to make him King in order to report to me every detail of their proposals. Now you can see why I decided your marriage to Abdel Sadek would be an excellent one for everyone concerned. Did you say he was fifty-two years old?"

"Yes!" Her voice was still emphatic with hurt and resentment.

"I believe he is only fifty-one. I suppose it is natural for you to think of him as too elderly for you. I can understand how a virgin of nineteen, particularly one who has no doubt discussed love with Western virgins, would dream of sharing her life with someone nearer her own age. It is deplorable if you have allowed such considerations to blind you to the advantages a young Muslim wife has when she is truly loved by a husband who is fifty-one. She can enjoy the most happy physical relations with such a man. Moreover, one of Abdel Sadek's age would treasure your affection more than a younger man. He would protect it by constant concern for your happiness. I have thought of these things, my dear child, and believe that instead of cruelty you will receive tenderness. Do you see now how idle your fears have been?"

"No! There are other things I know about him, Uncle Sajjid, which have nothing to do with his age."

Sajjid sighed. The girl was, of course, really frightened by her ignorant fears of marriage itself.

A scratching on the door precluded further discussion at the moment. Farha reached for her headdress. Sajjid opened the door sufficiently to hear the voice of the Clerk of Appointments.

"Professor Drench is here, Greatness. He says it is urgent."

"You may wait in the garden, Farha. We will resume when the professor has gone."

Sajjid promptly forgot Farha's unhappiness as Drench reported Newton's decision.

"But he arrived only yesterday, my uncle!"

"Nonetheless he says he must return at once."

"I will not permit it."

"I am afraid you are obliged to. The agreement you made stipulates that the time of his departure is entirely of his choosing."

"But the biography in the magazine described him as an honorable man. And in the short time he has been here my heart has warmed to him. Am I to believe that such a great scientist would accept my invitation merely for the money promised him? How could someone held so highly by his countrymen be the avaricious creature this action would prove him to be?"

"Wait, my nephew, wait! You are doing him an injustice. He feels, as I did, that a million dollars was an absurdly large fee to offer blindly. He declines to accept any of it.

"He *is* the honorable man we both thought him. He is also hypersensitive about accepting gifts. He asked me to return this with his deep appreciation of your generosity."

Sajjid stared at the *Parronde-Huissot* resting in its case.

"Yes, I know. I was as startled as you are. When I tried to dissuade him he was adamant. He even seemed reluctant to fly back in the plane that brought him, but when I pointed out that it would take at least two or three days to reach New York by way of Batrul Mina, he agreed to allow us to recall the Alitalia plane."

Sajjid at last closed his mouth.

"What did I do that offended him?"

"Nothing. It is simply that he is an extraordinary young man who feels strongly that he should return to New York as quickly as possible."

"Last night I made him leave the dinner with you while I sat with the *sheikhs* from Akhor. You are certain he is not angry with me?"

"I promise you he isn't. Not that I can tell you what prompted his decision, my nephew. I can only surmise that it relates to his forthcoming marriage. Yesterday he was unable to put through a telephone call to his fiancée. This morning, when I asked the palace switchboard if his call had yet been put through, they said it had not, but that a cable had come from America signed 'Rowena.' When I went to his apartment he was holding a cable in his hand. He invited me to read another which was a reply to one he had sent Thackaray Dynamics. It said that the experts will arrive to-morrow afternoon, bringing all they need with them. I asked if he had heard from his fiancée. He said, 'Yes, I've received a cable.' He glanced at the paper in his hand, but he didn't seem overjoyed at getting it. Perhaps he must return because of information it conveyed."

"I had hoped for so much from him." Sajjid sighed. "Do you think that now he will not come to the Room of the Secret?"

"Why not? I'm sure he considers himself at your disposal until he leaves. Do you wish Rome instructed to send the plane?"

"You are convinced he is determined to go?"

"Yes, my nephew."

"Give the instructions. Then we will go see this unhappy lover." Drench left the room.

In the garden Sajjid saw Farha and was touched. Her cheeks were still wet and her eyes closed as she stared into her hopelessness.

"I have no more time at the moment, my niece. Write the letter to your school. We will talk again when I have leisure."

Properly masked, Farha rushed through the halls and above to the harem. Grandmother must tell her all she knew about Abdel Sadek's first wife, the one who had been Grandmother's dear friend and who had endured so many heartless indignities from her husband until her brothers had forced him to grant her a divorce.

Jabil the Mat watched His Majesty come with *Ustaz* Drench and the American from the latter's apartment. If he tried to follow them down the corridor he would be seen. The trio went up the great stairway to the second landing. As soon as they were out of sight he would go to the American's chambers with the camera Zarh, the shoe dealer, had given him and take the pictures. If the royal party went into the secret room the egg shell he had been instructed to place under the rug at the door would be crushed.

Newton was relieved to find that the King had not been annoyed by his hasty decision to go home.

"We are sorry for you to leave so soonly, Misser Bemis, but you do know best. Professor Drench was been told the plane do come almost before you to be saying Jack Robinson. Is to be so, is not, Professor Drench?"

"Quite right. A three P.M. departure from Qam will land you in New York about sunset."

"Thank you."

They had come a considerable distance from Newton's room and were advancing down a long hallway. What was this "certain place for very private speaking" to which Sajjid was conducting him?

"The room we go to is being down there," said Sajjid pointing to the end of the corridor. Fifty steps more and the mystery would be ended.

"I'd like to say, sir," said Newton, "that I deeply appreciate all the consideration you have given me. I don't know what you're going to show me, but I doubt that in the little time I have left I can begin to merit your hospitality."

"Oh, no, Misser Bemis. I did to do nothing. Here we go in. But before so, please to answering a question." He queried Uncle Wex. "What is the name of the book of *khurafas?*"

"In English, it is called *The Arabian Nights.*"

"Right ho. You know this *Arabian Nights* book, Misser Bemis?"

"I've read parts of it."

"Jolly good. You know this great Caliph Haroun-al-Rashid?

‡ 143 ‡

What he do to be helping Baghdad peoples?"

"I remember the story vaguely, sir."

"He do go amongst Baghdad peoples like—*Man houa al-in-gleezi allazi youktherou min ad-aselah?*"

"Nosy Parker?" Drench ventured.

"Yes, yes. Nosy Parker. *Haroun-al-Rashid* do go everywhere to learning what is happen. I speak to me, 'Why not I do also what *Haroun-al-Rashid* doing so peoples of Suruk have fine things from Western World so to living in the pink?' I speak more to me, 'Not all things other countries have maybe top hole for Suruki peoples. When Program will be resuming every tomdickenarry will try making me to buy things. I do not to be buying—*samak fi l-bahr?*"

"Pig in a poke," translated Drench.

"Pig in poke. How I am to learn what are good? I do then think maybe I go to United States and see. But how can a king to do so? In United States every tomdickenarry say, 'Welcome, welcome, King Sajjid! Come buying this, come buying that.' Every persons try to selling pig in poke. So I do know I must to go like *Haroun-al-Rashid* not to be known by persons any place. What is word that mean how I do go?" This was to Drench.

"Incognito."

"Incognito. No person must to know I am Sajjid."

So that was why six months ago Mrs. Briscoe had to destroy those photograph negatives!

They had been standing before a locked door which the King himself opened. A wide screen a few feet within prevented anyone in the hall from seeing the room's contents. Sajjid pressed a switch. Lights flooded the part of the room behind the screen. Sajjid slid into its slot a protective bolt on the door.

"Now, Misser Bemis, I do show how I making me incognito in United States. Come, please."

It was as well-equipped a soda fountain as Newton had ever seen. Sajjid had slipped into a white jacket and was spreading a magazine open on the counter.

"You are knowing this magazine, Misser Bemis? He is *U.S. Syrup Dealer.*"

"No, I don't sir."

"Is fine teaching for many kinds fountain specialities; sundaes, fruit combos—combos are meaning combinations—and et cetera. I also do studying *The Fountaineer.* The magazine called *Short* say you do work to soda fountain in Granton. So maybe you are knowing *Fountaineer?*

"No, sir, I never saw it. And we didn't have many specialties."

"You do not to make malteds?"

"Oh, yes. Malteds, milk shakes, and sundaes."

Sajjid laughed. "Maybe then I do knowing many more of kinds than you. What you liking I am to make?"

Two hours later, Newton had corrected some of Sajjid's errors in following *The Fountaineer's* recipes. His honest approval of one of Sajjid's own creations, a fruit *frappé,* dusted with candied violets, pleased Sajjid greatly. When the coaching and corrections were completed, Newton elated his pupil by acknowledging the possibility that after an apprenticeship in sandwich and salad making and an intensified study of English, he might be able to familiarize himself with Americans at a grass-roots level. Drench's protest that he himself could not tell one sweet drink from another, had obliged Newton to judge Sajjid's qualification as a soda jerk.

"I believe I was the first man," Newton told Timmy later, "ever to sample thirty-two sodas and sundaes in the interest of the State Department."

Chapter 13

"When does Dolly want us?" asked Sir Tertius.

"Seven," said Lady Hipp. "But there won't be a guest of honor."

"What's happened?"

"Mr. Bemis has gone back."

"Gone back? What do you mean? The man got here yesterday."

"Gone back in the sense of having returned somewhere. In this case, to his home, the United States of America."

Sir Tertius lifted his eyes from checking the *Daily Telegraph* crossword solution.

"Think of that. Rather short stay, what?"

"Go back to your puzzle, dear."

Sir Tertius considered the situation. "That's a bit odd of him, isn't it?"

Beryl did not reply.

He asked again, "That's a bit odd of him, isn't it?" He saw that Beryl was not present. Well, he would probably hear more about it later. One could never tell what a Yank might do. Sir Tertius resumed his study of the solution. By God, he'd been right! *Laban gets confused in short streets* (2, 6) had been partly an anagram!

After memorizing Zarh, the shoe dealer's, information, Awadh hurried through the *suq* and sped rapidly along the road from Qam. Remembering the Ambassador's warning he pedaled more slowly as he approached the legation compound.

"Yes?" snapped Boris Voronsky. He had just received another prompting from Moscow to follow Bemis' every move.

"I have the report, Excellency. This morning the American went into the secret room with His Majesty and Professor Drench."

"How long did they stay?"

"They were there two hours."

"Continue."

"That is all, Excellency."

"Where is the camera with the pictures of all the papers in the American's rooms?"

"Jabil says—"

"I have told you never to mention the names of individuals."

"Forgive, Excellency. The person at the palace says the person at the shoe shop did not give him film to put in the camera. That is true, Excellency. You gave me none to give to the person at the shoe shop."

Voronsky exploded.

"What a fool! The film was already in the camera. Hurry back and tell the person in the *suq* all one has to do is follow the instructions, merely to turn the little knob after each picture. When he has taken thirty-six, to bring the camera back to the *suq*. No, *you* wait there and give our palace friend the instructions yourself when he makes his afternoon report."

"I obey, Excellency."

When the door closed behind Awadh, Voronsky tried to weigh Jabil's bulletin without bursting into tears of rage at this latest proof of his imbecility. He heard Natasha's knock on the door.

"Forgive me, Boris, but Dolly wants to know if we can come to dinner this evening."

Voronsky gulped. "To meet the American?"

"He will not be there."

"Not be there?"

"That is what she said."

Well, think of that! The missile discussions must be complex if Bemis cannot dine with his country's ambassador!

"Did Mrs. Briscoe say why?"

"Yes. He flew home to America an hour ago."

"What did he say, my nephew?" Sajjid's dejection aroused Drench's sympathy.

"He declined it, too."

"When you reconsider it you will recognize that it was not a gift he could possibly accept. You saw what had to be done to the runway of your own airport to allow the jet to land."

"I told him if he would not accept the big one which he admitted he liked, it could be a very small one that would land anywhere. There must be airports near Granton. It is mortifying that I cannot discharge the obligation of a host."

"He will surely be happy to keep the chess set. It's one that not even Mr. Bemis would not consider too magnificent to accept."

"It is absurdly trivial. I wanted him to have a keepsake worthy of my position. A king with the wealth God has given me would not give a chess set only a blind man might think worth buying in the beggar's *suq*."

Chapter 14

Having gotten to Rome without a fight, Mrs. Madge Wisser was determined not to let Morty Ockerman get her goat now.

"I would appreciate your taking one of me here, Morty," she said patiently, smiling at the girl behind the souvenir counter.

"Look, Mrs. Wisser, they've called the plane twice. They're very kindly holding it so I can get one of you at the bar. I already got you buying souvenirs at Honolulu, Tokyo, Bangkok, and Athens. I gotta get one of you at a foreign bar. Those are my instructions, so it's gotta be here. Please, Mrs. Wisser, play ball with me. You said you'd co-operate."

"All in good time. I'm obliged to purchase something at each stop." Mrs. Wisser resumed considering the figurine of the two babies being suckled by a coyote or something. At first it had seemed in bad taste. Still it was touching too, and the girl said it was very famous and everybody would know it was from Rome.

"For God's sake, Mrs. Wisser."

"How much?"

"Eighteen hundred *lira,* Signora. Three dollars."

"All righty. I'll take two." She opened her purse. She might as well get rid of some of this crazy foreign money. "How much will that be in *dratchmas* and—what are these?"

"*Rupees,* Signora."

"Look, don't bother with that, Mrs. Wisser. Here's six dollars, lady."

"Why, thank you, Morty. That's very gracious of you." She made it sound as if she meant it. Of course it would go on his expense account. Fat chance of this Morty spending his own money on anyone.

"Forget it. It's my pleasure."

Morty looked at his light meter. The airport bar was in line with the souvenir stand and getting the same amount of sun. He would use the Rolly.

The girl was putting the first little statue in a box.

"I'd like one of them gift-wrapped, please."

"I'll gift-wrap both, Signora."

"Look, lady," snapped Morty, "just put them both in a bag." He stopped Mrs. Wisser before she could give him one of her looks. "We'll get it gift-wrapped in New York. Exactly the way you want it. O.K.? Do it fast, lady. We'll come back and pick them up in a minute. Look, Mrs. Wisser, they've called the plane twice. Please let's get the hell to the bar."

Mrs. Wisser decided it was time for a showdown. Up to now, she had managed not to be taken while drinking. All too well she remembered Fred and the camera girl in the café that time in Tijuana. The girl had made Fred so mad he'd almost busted her camera because of the impression it might make if he was seen holding a highball by Mr. Hilder or any of the other officers at the bank. If the Dan Ringhalter Show let her be seen on TV sitting on a stool in front of all those bottles it could easily affect Fred's job. And even if it didn't it would get Fred so mad she would want to die.

"Morty, I know you must do your work, but nothing was said in the agreement about my drinking at bars."

His temper was wearing thin but Morty kept cool.

"Mrs. Wisser, the program has an Eyetalian vermouth sponsor and it's essential that I get a shot of you enjoying some. It will be stated that's what you're imbibing and nobody can take offense. It's practically a soft drink."

"All vermouth is a combination of several wines and herbs. I happen to have heard the commercial many, many times."

"All right. Lemme check." He consulted his list. "O.K. Quenchy's a sponsor, too. Everybody knows Quenchy's a completely soft drink. You can be holding a Quenchy bottle. I'll get the bartender to put the vermouth in front of that gentleman there and it will look like that's the beverage he's having. O.K.?"

Well, if Morty was fooling her, there could be big trouble. On the other hand, when she'd protested as the wife of a trustee of the Reformed Church of God that she should not be seen in that heathen temple in India or wherever it was, Morty had pointed out that respect for her religious feelings was nowhere in the contract and she might have to forfeit the five thousand dollars when she completed the Dan Ringhalter You Win Tour. The funny look in his eye suggested he was going to bring the subject up again.

"How do you know they have Quenchy?"

"The least we can do is go see. Look, Mrs. Wisser, if they don't have Quenchy, you can be drinking Commodore Whiteman's Lemon Delight. I can see a bottle of it even from here. Let's go, huh?"

"Very well, as soon as I get a post card."

"For crissake, Mrs. Wisser, we'll be back in L.A. before the card could get there!"

"Please don't touch my sleeve again, Morty. Thank you, miss. You wrap very nicely. What is this one of?" Mrs. Wisser was at the post card rack.

"The Quirinale Palace, Signora. Fifteen cents."

"Would you see it got mailed?"

"Of course, Signora. With stamp it will be—"

"Look, Mrs. Wisser." Was she trying to make him blow his top? "I'm asking you for the last time—"

‡ 151 ‡

"Morty!" Mrs. Wisser had had about all she could take. "I am required to send Mr. Ringhalter a post card from each and every place visited. If you will look at the agreement—."

The third and last call over the loudspeaker specifically named passengers Ockerman and Wisser. Morty saw the airline man hurrying toward them.

"Mr. Ockerman, I can't hold the plane any longer. If you and Mrs. Wisser don't run, you won't be able to board."

"Just a second," said Mrs. Wisser. Each card had to have a different greeting on it, so that when Mr. Ringhalter read it to the studio audience, it wouldn't be what she'd said on the one before.

This is Italy's royal palace and very impressive indeed. Now off to the good old U.S.A. Cheerily.

Madge Wisser.

"How much is the stamp, dear?" The girl was watching the Signora's companion tagging after the One World Airways station manager, pleading. Mrs. Wisser looked in their direction, too.

"I'm sorry, Mr. Ockerman. I know you are expected to travel by One World and receive special attention. I've tried to give it. I delayed the flight for more than ten minutes, but there were other important passengers on it, too." He tried to appear sympathetic as he waited for Morty's reaction.

"When's the next plane?"

"For our next flight to New York you'd have to wait six hours, and right now that's completely booked. Pan American has one leaving in about forty minutes. Shall I try to get you on that?"

"Yes, please."

The OWA man hurried away.

Morty started back to Mrs. Wisser. She was fishing in her bag for money for the stamp. He continued past her to the bar. Grimly, he slipped the straps off his shoulders and rested his cameras on the stool beside him.

"What's the strongest brandy you got?" he asked the barman.

"You wish cognac?"

"Cognac, brandy, anything." If the One World guy didn't see that they arrived at the studio tomorrow morning it could be curtains for Morty on the Dan Ringhalter Show. They'd have to accept Mrs. Wisser's getting sick and costing him two days in Bombay as an Act of God; he could show them the doctor's certificate. And they might overlook coming from Rome to New York by another line if One World picked them up at Kennedy and took them to L.A. But losing a whole day in Japan because she couldn't make up her mind about those damn kimonos and another in Hong Kong on account of whatever the hell it was she was buying should have tipped him off to what to expect from her. After all, he was supposed to make her stick to the schedule. If he got canned it might count against him on the whole network. If it hadn't been for this dame, this would have been the best assignment yet. What a kook!

He ordered another brandy.

The telephone on the desk of the Alitalia station manager interrupted his duty as a host.

"Excuse me, Mr. Bemis." He lifted the receiver.

"Yes? . . . Put him on, please . . . Yes, Joe? . . . Hold on. I'll see." He flicked the switch to the line's clearance office. "*Sul del sei tre due*: *c'e posto in prima? . . . Grazie.*" He returned to the caller on the telephone. "Not even a single in tourist, Joe . . . I'll be glad to, but I doubt that there will be . . . Right." He hung up.

"Everyone wants to go to New York today." He smiled. "Yours is the only plane leaving Rome with two passengers."

"Only one, this trip."

The station manager looked at Newton uncertainly then picked up the PIL sheet for the chartered flight.

"I have two passengers listed on your manifest. You and a Mrs. Haruba." He passed the sheet to Newton.

"There's some mistake. Mrs. Haruba expected to be with me, but she stayed in Qam. Who made this check against her name?"

"The ramp supervisor at Qam. May I see the sheet again?" Newton returned it. "Ah, this may explain it. You have two bedrooms. She must be resting. I was about to ask if I couldn't offer her some refreshment."

A call from the dispatcher informed him that Mr. Bemis' plane was ready to depart.

King Sajjid's fountain drinks had destroyed any desire Newton might have had for lunch. He still felt a bit queasy. The station manager invited him to have a drink at the airport bar, and Newton asked for some bicarbonate of soda. As the barman prepared it a man with a collection of camera gear on the seat beside him spoke to another who had just approached.

"So what gives?"

"Nothing, I'm afraid. I've contacted every other line with afternoon departures but there isn't a single seat available. At the moment the best I can guarantee you is our Flight 664."

"What time does that get to New York?"

"Ten-thirty A.M., New York time. At Kennedy International we can put you on our Flight 82 to Los Angeles. You should arrive there at two P.M. California time."

Morty groaned inwardly. The OWA man turned to his Alitalia colleague.

"What about your Milan-New York flight, Guido? Maybe I can get them on BEA to Milan."

"That's full, too. I had requests on it half an hour ago."

Overhearing Morty Ockerman's predicament and the helplessness of the airline men prompted Newton to make a suggestion which led to a major change in his plans for the future.

Chapter 15

The stewardess who met Newton at the plane's entrance seemed surprised that he had not been aware Mrs. Haruba was traveling with him. She had come aboard at Qam shortly after the jet had arrived and said she would like to sleep until they left Rome. Would Mr. Bemis like her to be wakened?

"No, let her sleep." No doubt the King had kept her so busy she was as tired as he had been when he arrived from New York.

Newton resumed reading the report of NASA's Dr. Hermann J. Schaeffer on the problem of solar flares. It was encouraging to learn they could now be fairly well predicted up to four days in advance by astronomers specializing in the sun. Encouraging, but not good enough for men on lunar missions. Not when the electrical activity caused by charged proton particles entering human bodies could damage the intestinal tract and bone marrow. A superconductive metal like niobium could offer a bit of magnetic field armor against both solar and cosmic radiation, but its effectiveness would be relative. When the sun went on that five-day rampage in November, 1960, it saturated space with lethally charged cores of hydrogen atoms. Men in space then would have been dead within two weeks after their exposure. If future protons were of low energy, the chance of surviving a flare might be good. But even if the eruption from the sun only sickened the selenauts, the fact remained that the first projected half-million-mile round trip to the moon would take eight days. Therefore the astronomers' predictions would have to be extended four days to provide a margin of safety.

"Are you Mr. Bemis?"

The smile of the woman standing in the aisle was meant to be ingratiating. She must be the companion of the man being relieved of his camera equipment by the steward. Politely, Newton rose.

"Yes, ma'am."

"I want to thank you kindly for your very sweet gesture." She tilted her head to one side to emphasize the sincerity with which she was extending her right hand.

"I'm Mrs. Madge Wisser. My husband is Mr. Fred Wisser of the Union First National of Azusa, California. Oh, would you put those back on one of the seats? I want to get at them in a while." The stewardess holding an armful of Mrs. Wisser's belongings took them to the rear of the plane.

Though eager to get back to Dr. Schaeffer, Newton tried not to make his responsive how-do-you-do too curt and failed to curb Mrs. Wisser's sociability. As he was still standing, Mrs. Wisser said, "Pray sit down," and snuggled herself into the lounge seat opposite his. Morty joined them. He'd had no chance to tell Mrs. Wisser they were not to bother the guy. Just get on the plane and leave him alone.

"Where would you like us to sit?" asked Morty. Mrs. Wisser blandly appraising their host failed to note the hint in his voice.

"Anywhere you'd like," said Newton, "there are plenty of seats." Morty looked at Mrs. Wisser.

"Let's go back and pick out a couple, huh?" This time he spoke pointedly.

Momentarily free of Morty's domination, Mrs. Wisser offered a counterthrust.

"I'm talking with Mr. Bemis at the moment, Morty."

Morty felt all he could do was clam up. "O.K." He went to a seat in the rear of the plane.

"Where is your home, Mr. Bemis?"

"In New York." Maybe brief answers would modify her effusiveness.

"For goodness sake! Mr. Wisser's sister resides in New York. You may know her husband, Judge Norris Cavanaugh? When he retired last year he was urged to run for Congress but declined."

"I'm afraid I've not met him."

"A very fine man. Are you with the airline, Mr. Bemis?"

"No, I just happen to be traveling alone."

"Oh. And may I ask where you've come from?"

"I've been in the Middle East." Being laconic wasn't helping much. Perhaps she was extending the conversation more as a rebuff to the man with the cameras than because of habitual nosiness.

"Would you care to guess where I've come from?"

"Perhaps you'd better tell me."

"When I get back to Los Angeles, I will have been around the whole world. Are you familiar with the Dan Ringhalter Show?"

"I'm afraid not."

"Well, it's on at ten-thirty A.M. in L.A. and they have this You Win contest on Tuesdays. The way it's worked is Mr. Ringhalter comes down among the audience and takes your name and then he flips a lot of cards right in front of you and whenever you want to you say 'Stop!' and wherever he stops is what you win. Well, it just so happened I said 'Stop!' right after a card that would have given me a beautiful freezer. Well, of course, the next card after a handsome prize like that is usually some dinky thing, like one of Mr. Ringhalter's albums or something. I guess I was a little provoked at having missed the freezer. Anyway, that's when I said 'Stop,' without realizing it had slipped out. My friend who'd come with me said, 'Oh, Madge, you shouldn't have!' and I was about to say I couldn't agree with her more and then I looked at Mr. Ringhalter. His hand was covering the card. He said, 'Well, Mrs.

Wisser, it seems you've won a girdle.' Well, everybody laughed and of course I had to laugh, too, because after all it is just a game and then Mr. Ringhalter said, 'Yes, sir, you've won a girdle!' And right then the big bell rang. Well, the big bell rings only when the big prize of the day had been won by somebody. So I thought, 'Why, what on earth does he mean?' And Mr. Ringhalter says, 'Yes, Mrs. Wisser, it seems you've won a girdle but it's a girdle you're going to make yourself. It happens to be a girdle you are going to make around the earth! You have just won a three-weeks' global tour on One World Airways, the Executive Height of World Wide Flight.' Well, of course, I couldn't believe my ears and then, as if that wasn't enough, he said besides having all my expenses paid I would receive five thousand dollars if I showed up at the studio four Tuesdays hence, the idea being that I'd have a week to prepare for the trip. So, lo and behold, here I am, homeward bound, tired but happy." She paused so that Newton could fully digest her astounding achievement.

Newton did his best. "Let me congratulate you."

For four weeks Mrs. Wisser's audiences had accustomed her to gasps of astonishment and demands for more details. The way this man acted you'd think she'd won a box of cake mix.

Newton sensed her discomfiture. "Is your husband enjoying the trip?"

"Oh, that's not Mr. Wisser, alas. That gentleman's with the show. He came along to make photographs of me on tour. Mr. Wisser was entitled to come along, but unfortunately the bank found it impossible to let him go at this time. Then I was told I could take anyone I wanted so I asked Mrs. Loffing, the lady I mentioned was with me. She's a dear friend and she was all set to come along but an hour before we were to leave her asthma come back on her and her doctor absolutely put his foot down on her going anywhere."

"What a pity."

"Yes, it was. So it turned out I had to do the whole thing single-handed. However, I must say it was quite an experience."

"I can well believe it."

Mr. Bemis certainly didn't give out much. Mrs. Wisser made one more effort to be nice to him.

"At each stop I was required to purchase something that showed I'd been there. Would you care to see some of my trophies?"

"I wouldn't want you to open your luggage."

"Oh, I have most of them back there on my seat in what I call my 'loot bag.'" Her chortle made it clear that 'loot bag' was a joke. "It's really quite a lovely carryall which Mr. Ringhalter gave me with his compliments."

"Will you fasten your seat belts, please?" The stewardess continued to the rear to let the other unexpected passenger know they were about to take off.

"When I finish reading this, perhaps I can come back and look at them."

Despite the smiling way he said it, it was clear he wanted her to leave him. She did so abruptly. Whatever business Mr. Bemis might be in, he was certainly a cold fish. She retreated to where the girl had put her things. Morty was looking at a magazine two rows behind. That was all right with her. The less she saw of that one the pleasanter it would be.

Who was Mr. Bemis? If he wasn't with the airline, what was he doing with a whole plane to himself? So he'd come from the Middle East. That might mean Turkey or Greece or somewhere like that. Maybe he was one of those fabulously rich ship owners like the man whose yacht they had seen anchored off Athens or someplace. Or he could be a millionaire tycoon like Howard Hughes with interests all over. Well, if he came back she'd just ask him. What were those two compartment-like things facing each other a little ways up front? Each took up the space of four seats and had a door like it was a room. Maybe that's what they were: bedrooms. Whoever he was, this Mr. Bemis certainly traveled in style. Well, he was in no hurry to come see the souvenirs so she might as well try to catch up with her journal. Having to do the whole trip in three weeks had allowed only one day in some countries and that didn't give much time to study the natives and jot down the local color like Mr. Ringhalter's assistant had requested her to do. She got out her little book and then looked in all three bags for the OWA route map that showed all the places she had been. She couldn't find it. My goodness, had she lost another one? It would be embarrassing to have to ask that Morty to make the lines on a third one. She reread her Hong Kong notes. They were sketchy but then the hotel bill-of-fares were probably with the other menus in the big suitcases in the baggage compartment, and later she could fill in what they ate there. Or was that the place where they had dined on the floating restaurant the OWA man had taken them to and she'd forgot to take a menu? All right, she would write about how all the poor people lived on boats. That was Hong Kong, wasn't it? Or was it one of those places in India or in Bombay? Oh, well, she could straighten that out later, too, because wherever it was there was a picture of it on one of the post cards. Turning a page in the book she encountered an entry marked *Bangok*. It was blank. Oh, dear, she had failed to put down any impressions about it. Bangok? Bangok? Which country was that in? She tapped her head gently with her pencil. Her struggle to remember was halted by the opening of the door to one of the rooms. A girl stuck her head out. She was leaning into the aisle as if she didn't want to be seen, and, as she was peering up ahead, Mrs. Wisser couldn't see her face. The two-piece ensemble she was wearing looked like the French import one of the models wore last month on that TV fashion show. After a moment, she stepped all the way out and walked kind of timidly towards the lounge. If she was looking for Mr. Bemis, she'd have to go up front because he was in a lounge seat next to the window. The girl stopped and for a second just stood there, hesitating. She clenched her fists at her sides as if it was hard for her to make up her mind. Then she turned around, her eyes on the floor and started back. When she got to the door of the room she looked up and saw Mrs. Wisser. Mrs. Wisser had never seen anybody look more surprised than the girl did. Was she deciding whether to say hello or not? All of a sudden she hurried back into the room. By leaning out into the aisle, Mrs. Wisser saw the sliding door of the room close again. That was certainly peculiar. She and Morty were supposed to be the only people on the plane besides Mr. Bemis. She stood up and looked back at where Morty was. He was still reading his magazine and had missed the whole thing. She sat down again.

The girl was kind of pretty in a foreign way. She was probably Mrs. Bemis. Why was she acting like she was scared to go up and join her husband? Maybe they'd had a fight and she didn't know how to get him to make up. It might be very tough, married to a man like Mr. Bemis. Just talking to him you could see how icy he could be. If his wife said anything he didn't like he might snap her head off. Men could have awful cruel streaks in them. The girl was quite young. Maybe they'd just got married. Could she be his sister, maybe? It didn't seem likely with him so tall and long-faced and her being so pretty and with such a cute figure. His secretary maybe? If so, she was very pretty for one. Surely she wasn't a chippy. She looked too refined to be. Still and all, rich men often . . .

The stewardess coming from the place up where they kept dishes and things halted Mrs. Wisser's speculations. The stewardess stopped at the room the girl was in and knocked. The girl must have rung for her. The stewardess slid the door open and went in. Mrs. Wisser listened but she couldn't hear the conversation in the room. Maybe she could if she sort of strolled past the open door. If anybody saw her, she could go on up to one of the toilets. She was rising from her seat when the stewardess came out and closed the door behind her.

"Oh, Miss!" The stewardess came to her chair.

"Yes, Signora. May I get you something?"

"I was just wondering who that young lady in there is."

"Her name is Mrs. Haruba."

"Beg pardon?"

"Mrs. Haruba. She is a Suruki lady."

"A what?"

"A Suruki lady. She is from Suruk. She is with Mr. Bemis."

"Oh, I see. Well, thank you."

The stewardess smiled and went up front again. Mrs. Wisser saw her stop at the lounge where Mr. Bemis was sitting. Before you could count ten Mr. Bemis was in the aisle, heading for the room. He knocked on the door. As it slid open, Mrs. Wisser watched a funny expression come on his face as he stared into the room. She heard him say, "Where's Mrs. Haruba?" She couldn't hear what the girl said back, but, after standing there a moment with his mouth open, Mr. Bemis went in. The seat in front of Mrs. Wisser's was right behind the bedroom so she switched. She could hear a little better but couldn't make out what they were saying. She leaned out again and peered around the partition. As the stewardess was moving about up front, Mrs. Wisser didn't dare stretch her head any closer to the open door. There was nothing to do but sit back and let on like she wasn't concerned.

At first, Newton was dumbfounded; as he listened he began finding the girl's story curiously consistent with other incredibilities of his Suruki visit. A more objective observer than himself might have suspected that Sajjid's humanitarian zeal was more capricious than habitual. Identifying herself had been unnecessary. Her voice had the same harplike grace so noticeable in the Gardens of Beautiful Deceit. The masked Farha's statement that she was nineteen was confirmed by the flower freshness of the girl's face.

"My uncle was distressed that nothing he had offered you had found favor in your eyes. When Professor Drench told him you had been pleased with my services he decided, inadequate though I was, I would be the only souvenir from Qam you would possibly accept. And to prevent you hastily rejecting me, he had me put aboard without your knowledge, with instructions that I not disclose myself until the plane had left Rome.

"I am sorry I know nothing of the United States except what I have read and learned from my American schoolmates. But I have been told I am bright and if you and the lady you are marrying

‡ 162 ‡

can be patient with me, surely I can become useful to you both in a short time. Should you decide to use me as a secretary I will study shorthand and whatever else is necessary to make me helpful. I would, of course, expect no wages. My uncle would provide whatever money I needed. If in time you found me burdensome, I would be prepared for dismissal. All my uncle asks is that you give him and me the opportunity to prove my acceptability. You are saying nothing. Am I rejected?"

Newton found some words. "It is a bit difficult to believe what I'm hearing. You, a girl with intelligence and—well, with a Western education—you can think of yourself as a 'souvenir,' a piece of property with no authority over your own actions. My God, what about your wedding, your affection for the man you've been expecting to marry?"

"It is kind of you to consider my personal feelings. But I do not feel I have been deprived of a husband I loved. I have never seen the man who was my fiancé. My uncle, as the King, has the power to cancel the engagement. And I am happy to obey his command."

"But if I agreed to accept you as a gift—I suppose I really am awake and facing such a situation—how could you possibly hope to enter the United States?"

"I have a passport which will allow me to come to America as a student. There is no reason for anyone to know that our relationship is that of master and slave."

A gasp in the aisle outside the room made Newton look out. Mrs. Wisser was weaving her way back to where the photographer was sitting, holding the backs of seats for support. Possibly the woman was ill.

"Can I help you, Mrs. Wisser?" Newton asked.

Mrs. Wisser halted and faced the man who was no longer an enigma. She had distinctly heard the girl's admission. For once, Mrs. Wisser was without words. She managed to shake her head in response to his question, wheel about, and continue staggering back until she sank into the seat beside Morty's.

Watching her move away, Newton wondered if Mrs. Wisser

might be a dipsomaniac. He had seen that kind of bewildered stare before on the faces of suddenly incapacitated drunks. His concern returned to a more important quandary. Any effort he might make to free this wretched girl from her spineless submissiveness was likely to be futile. If her teachers in Switzerland had failed, what could he hope to achieve? When he rejoined her, she was smiling and offering him a small package.

"It is from my uncle. Another souvenir, perhaps."

It had been hastily wrapped in a square of white silk and tied with string. Farha exclaimed joyfully as she saw its contents.

"Oh, Mr. Bemis, my uncle must be very fond of you! It is a chess set he himself made years ago. When I was very young he gave me my first lessons with those pieces."

The wooden figures had been carved a bit crudely but were clearly identifiable, and the squares on the small folding board were meticulously symmetrical. Sajjid must have read every word of the article in *Short!* If only he had limited his farewell gifts to this touching memento.

"Do you play, Mr. Bemis?"

"Quite a bit." He had decided what to do about Farha. In Washington he would turn her over to Ambassador Hunain with expressions of regret.

They talked chess. Each disclaimed having more than ordinary competence.

"What do I think? I think it sounds screwy." Morty would have told Mrs. Wisser he also thought she was screwy if she hadn't been white as a sheet. Maybe she was nuts at that. "You're certain she said it?"

"I am not deaf, Morty."

"Tell me exactly what you heard."

Mrs. Wisser was able to keep her voice low and comparatively steady.

"I was right outside the door, as close as I am to you, and I heard her say they could get away with it because she had a passport that would make people think she was a student and that nobody would know she actually was a slave."

Morty pondered. "They must have been kidding."

"Did you see him rush out when he suspected I'd heard? 'Can I help you, Mrs. Wisser?'" Mrs. Wisser put her hands over her heart, it was fluttering so. "Oh, boy!"

"Did you get a good look at her?"

"Not very close but she looks Oriental. She's supposed to be a married woman from Suruk. Were we in Suruk?"

"No." Morty produced the flight map and examined a page revealing a large part of the Middle East. "Wait a second. Look!"

Mrs. Wisser looked and clapped a hand to her mouth.

"Yep, it's an Arabian country," said Morty. "That's where there's still harems and slaves, too!" His resistance to this kooky dame's story was lessening. What if she really had stumbled onto something? Was this Bemis mixed up in a racket nobody knew about? He pressed the button which would bring the stewardess.

"Let me ask the questions. Don't you say anything. It's important that nobody knows we're suspicious."

"Yes, sir?" asked the stewardess.

"Maybe you don't know it," said Morty, chattily, "but this lady and I are flying with you because we missed the plane we were supposed to be on. Is this somebody's private jet?"

"No, sir. It belongs to Alitalia. It is on a chartered flight."

"I see. Is Mr. Bemis the party we're to thank?"

"I don't know, sir. The plane was chartered by the King of Suruk. May I bring you something to drink?"

Mrs. Wisser's involuntary gasp demanded quick action.

"A drink might settle your stomach," Morty urged tactfully.

Mrs. Wisser regained control of her thoughts.

"What?"

"Your stomach. Maybe a little whiskey would help it."

"Oh, yes. Maybe it would." After a moment's consideration, Mrs. Wisser said she would have a Scotch old fashioned going easy on the sugar. Mrs. Wisser was silent until the girl was out of earshot.

"Well, what do you know!" whispered Mrs. Wisser.

Morty's voice also dropped a few decibels. "Yeah. *Very* interesting. Could it be our Mr. Bemis is *him?*"

"Who?"

"The King. She said she was *his* property, didn't she?"

"Yes, but what about his saying he lives in New York? And his talking like an American and all!"

"A lot of foreign rulers have gone to Harvard, haven't they?"

"Very true." Another retrospection presented itself. "But why did he look so surprised when he saw her?"

"It could have been an act."

"No, it couldn't have been. He didn't know I was watching. Wait. You know something?"

"What?"

"She could have got on board at Rome! This is a an Italian plane, isn't it?"

"So what?"

"Don't a lot of big underworld czars live in Italy? The ones mixed up with dope and call girls and everything?"

"Yeah, like old Lucky—"

"Sh!"

The King, or Mr. Bemis, or whoever he was, was coming out of the room with a box under his arm. The girl followed him up to the lounge.

In New York chess clubs Newton had occasionally found himself facing internationally known men players. Once or twice draws had sent him home astonished at his unexpected achievements. He had often wondered if his modest skill could win a draw against the legendary Miss Sonja Graf. Even before Newton had been born, Miss Graf had been considered the second-best woman player in the world. In the '50s she had four times won the U.S. Women's Open Championship, and in the Spring of '64 had regained the title. Newton had scrutinized her game-charts and was familiar with her frequently unorthodox openings and variations.

The jet had been less than five hours in flight when Newton wondered what chance Miss Graf would have if matched against the amazing violet-eyed girl opposite him. Like Miss Graf, this phenomenon had no patience for positional play. Four times she had effortlessly demolished all of his own rarely employed but almost invincible stratagems and left him gaping at the wreckage.

Yes, she admitted, Uncle Sajjid, whose skill she never hoped to equal, had occasionally found something in her game worth complimenting, but, of course, she would hesitate to challenge an acknowledged master.

"You seemed surprised that I decide my moves a bit faster than most players. I know it is a fault I should correct if I want to be really proficient. And while it is pleasant to hear your compliments, I promise you there were several moments in the third and fourth games when I was in great difficulty."

Chapter 16

Awadh was panting.

"What did I tell you about riding so fast?" thundered Voronsky.

"I felt I must reach your Excellency quickly. There is great disturbance at the palace. The Princess Farha has disappeared."

"Disappeared? How?"

"No one seems to know exactly. Jabil told Zarh, the shoemaker, that she is thought to have fled to Marbhein. The *askeri* there are searching for a date merchant who left Qam with his camels before dawn."

Voronsky's appetite was so whetted he forgot to berate the boy for mentioning two individuals by name.

"Go on."

"The Princess' mother arrived from the north two hours ago with the *Sheikh* Abdel Sadek and his suite. The *Sheikh* has come to wed the Lady Farha."

"I know that. Why are they so certain she has fled?"

"Ismail Bin Mahsin, the policeman, rooms at my mother's house. In the *suq* he told me the *zabtiye* have been ordered to question all women her height."

"Return to the *suq* and try to learn something more."

"I obey, Excellency." Voronsky halted the boy in the doorway.

"Yes, Excellency?"

"This time you may ride fast."

Voronsky hurried to the code room. Moscow must be informed immediately of the Princess Farha's affront to the proud and powerful tribal chief who had encouraged Boyschekov to think he might welcome Russia's offer of assistance.

In the garden of the American Embassy, Dolly Briscoe and Natasha Voronsky were playing samba. Natasha had completed two canastas and was counting her red 3's when Lady Hipp appeared, unexpectedly.

"Has either of you seen any strange girls about this compound?"

"Strange girls?" echoed Dolly.

"Actually, just one. She's nineteen and weighs about eight stone. One of the *zabtiye* just telephoned. He said she's not a criminal or at all dangerous; merely missing. As she speaks English and French, she might pop up here. He said she was well dressed. Do you suppose she could be a *houri* from one of the *harims?* I think I'll call Eustace Drench and try to find out." Dolly laughed.

"How could he be expected to know?"

"He hears more about what happens in Qam than you'd imagine. He often gives me delicious bits of gossip."

Two minutes later, Drench was guardedly trying to satisfy Beryl's curiosity.

"I'm sorry the zibbies rang you up. I hope they haven't been a nuisance."

"They were as polite as jam. Is she one of the royal wives?"

"I expect you'll learn in a few hours, but until it's announced I suggest you keep it a secret. Agreed?"

"Girl guide's honor."

"The child happens to be one of the King's young relatives. When her mother, who's a bit of a termagant, began howling that she was nowhere in the palace, H.M. allowed the police to look for the girl. Actually, he knew where she was, but didn't want her whereabouts to become public knowledge. I know the child; she's an unusually sweet youngster and was about to be married to a rather unpleasant *sharif*. Her mother doesn't like me, and suspected I'd helped the girl to run away from him. Being as much in the dark as the mother was, I did a bit of investigating on my own. It wasn't until ten minutes ago I learned what had really happened."

"Don't be tedious, Eustace. Where is she?"

"On the plane with Mr. Bemis. I'd been told the lady who'd come from Washington had gone back, too. But when I found her in H.M.'s waiting room I concluded it was the girl who'd boarded the plane. A moment before you telephoned, H.M. confirmed my suspicion. I must go, Beryl. The jilted bridegroom has just come in with fire in his eye."

Beryl put back the receiver and returned to the garden. Dolly was mixing the decks before shuffling.

"What did he say?"

"He wasn't there."

When Dolly presently began to re-deal, Beryl unhurriedly departed. Her news, she decided, fully warranted waking Tertius from his afternoon lie-down.

Half a world away Harvey Priest was speaking over another telephone, the interdepartmental one connected with Webster Harris' office.

"I'd go myself," said Priest, "but the Secretary's in New York and he wants me to run a Cyprus session here at three. I don't know how long it will last. Bemis is due at Kennedy about seven. Find out why he came back so soon."

"*D'accord.*"

Webster called Rowena.

Rowena said she was depressed. Newton's cable to her had been maddeningly brief, containing not a clue to why he had stayed in Qam less than twenty-four hours.

"All he said was that he would phone me on arrival."

"I see. Rowena, I'm going to Kennedy. If you'd like to come along, I'll get a Department pass for you and we'll meet him at the steps of the plane."

Rowena felt much better. She need not wait for Newton's presence in Washington to cancel once and for all his veto of her absolutely wonderful plans for the first Futurian dwelling. It would be good to have Webster as a buffer when straightening Newton out.

"Thank you, darling," she said. "Then, if you don't have to hurry back to Washington, we can all dine together."

Chapter 17

The sixth game was interrupted by the captain's announcement that they were over Boston with New York forty minutes ahead.

"America!" Farha pressed her nose against the glass like a child at a bakery window. "Will I see Vermont?"

"No, we're flying due south. Why does Vermont interest you?"

"It is the state I shall be living in."

Newton abandoned the last of the engaging fancies that had floated through his mind while they were playing: Farha triumphing over such renowned women players as Zenaida Huber, Sara Kaufman, Adele Goddard, and the teen-agers, Cecelia Rock and Kate Silars, whom Samuel Reshevsky, himself, said were so promising. How could he make Farha appreciate the absurdity of Sajjid's command? He could see now that she was essentially a sensitive and innocent girl. Handing her over to Dr. Hunain so peremptorily would be brutal. Such an eagerness to be in America was pathetic and appealing. A more humane way must be found for conditioning her to Western mores. Perhaps with Rowena's help the problem could be solved. She could look after Farha for a time and, with friendly advice, facilitate the poor thing's adjustment. Then, if she didn't wish to go to an American college, perhaps acceptable work could be found for her at Thackaray.

Farha was looking at him quizzically.

"Do you not have a house in Vermont? My uncle told me you did."

"He's right, but at present it's being remodeled. After I'm married let's hope you can see it."

"I love the pictures I've seen of New England dwellings. What is being done to yours?"

Newton described several of the alterations.

"You do not seem too happy. Do you now question the wisdom of the changes?"

"I have some doubts. I may be pleasantly surprised, of course."

"I hope you are. Will you tell me what the surrounding country is like?"

Farha closed her eyes, the more vividly to experience Mr. Bemis' recollections. She heard the choirs of birds on mornings in the Spring. She felt the tree-shadowed coolness of his pond on August afternoons; pictured maples exploding with Autumn's colors; and winter landscapes even lovelier than those which had enchanted her at Montreux.

"I can ski," glowed Farha. Newton found that easy to believe. He could see her flying down Morgan's Hill, frost on her breath, her cheeks apple-red. The girl was truly remarkable.

The plane was pivoting slowly to a halt. Morty rebriefed Mrs. Wisser.

"Now, remember, just tell him 'Thanks a lot' and make for the door. Do it quick, but don't race or show you're nervous. I'll meet you in Immigration after I get a shot of them leavin' the plane."

Mrs. Wisser, festooned with bundles and bags, suddenly appeared at the lounge. Newton had completely forgotten the two extra passengers in the rear.

"I'd like to thank you very kindly for your courtesy." Mrs. Wisser might have been thanking a racking dentist. Newton assured her he was happy to have been helpful. He hoped the flight had not been uncomfortable.

"Oh, I feel just fine," she said stiffly. She did not trust herself to look at his companion. "Good-bye!"

The stewardess was holding more of her portable belongings. Mrs. Wisser wavered.

"Mr. Ockerman can take them. And thank you very much." Mrs. Wisser moved to the doorway.

The stewardess watched the heavily encumbered Mr. Ockerman making his way forward and wondered how he could possibly take on any more cargo.

Her heart pounding, Mrs. Wisser emerged on the landing platform and waddled down the steps.

Rowena looked questioningly at the airline official who had come with her and Webster to the apron. "It's the wrong plane!"

"No, it is Mr. Bemis'," he said reassuringly. "Rome notified us there would be three other passengers." He consulted the names on his teletyped PIL. The Mrs. Haruba listed was, of course, the Suruki lady whom he had seen off with Mr. Bemis forty-eight hours ago. The woman struggling with her bundles must be the one who had boarded the plane at Rome. He smiled, politely.

"Welcome home, Mrs. Wisser." Astonishingly, the woman froze in her tracks. Perhaps he had confused her. "I am with Alitalia," he explained.

Mrs. Wisser was seized by inner panic. The white slaver had seen her listening at that door and radioed ahead to have her rubbed out! She knew she must keep cool.

"Don't touch me!" she screamed.

Rowena watched the hysterical woman clutch her baggage as though menaced by footpads and dash for dear life to the incoming passenger entrance. Next Rowena saw a man, laden with impedimenta but unflustered, descend from the plane. At the foot of the steps he lowered all he was carrying onto the concrete and selected one of several cameras. Was he waiting to photograph Newton? She looked at the two men with her. Both were perplexed. Newton appeared in the doorway. He waved a greeting to Rowena and Webster. Rowena blew him a kiss. Her hand stayed in the air as a not unattractive girl joined him. As the two started down the steps, a steward and stewardess came behind with hand luggage.

Halfway to the ground the quartet was stopped by Morty's "Hold it, Mr. Bemis!"

"I'm an American citizen and I know what I'm talking about. I've been with them all the way from Rome!"

Betty Mae Hacklyn was used to dealing with agitated travelers, arriving home after months, sometimes a mere few weeks, abroad. She knew that the excitement of returning often produced a mild, momentary hysteria. As one of the Immigration Services's welcoming hostesses, it was part of her job to see that their passports and health certificates were in sight before directing them to the inspection booth.

"Wouldn't you like to sit down and rest a moment?" suggested Betty Mae. "I know what it is to be upset and . . ."

"Look, young lady, if somebody don't go out there and arrest them, they'll get away!"

"No, they won't," Betty Mae said soothingly. "If you'll look outside, you'll see there is no exit except through here."

Mrs. Wisser had no desire to go outside again. She scurried to a windowed booth in which an examiner was waiting.

Although disconcerted by the photographer's cheek—he was still snapping away—Newton introduced Farha as complaisantly as he could. Webster's greeting to her contained exactly the right combination of cordiality and deference. Alitalia's Mr. D'Angelo hoped the Princess' flight had been smooth. Rowena's mask was a reasonable facsimile of the face of a charmed fiancée as she learned that the Princess was visiting America for the first time and momentarily undecided on whether or not to continue her education here. The mask stayed on even when Rowena's eager concern was interrupted by an Immigration Service officer.

"May I speak to you, Mr. Harris?" The man stood a few feet away.

"Excuse me." Webster detached himself from the group.

"It's quite all right, Harris," said the Secretary. "The Trusteeship meeting adjourned ten minutes ago and I'm across the street at our Mission office."

"Can you speak freely, sir?"

"No one is here I can't trust." The Secretary smiled at Ambassador Adlai Stevenson. "Go ahead."

"I'm at Kennedy International, sir. Mr. Priest instructed me to meet Mr. Newton Bemis' plane from Suruk. As you perhaps know, Mr. Bemis is a scientist who's been visiting King Sajjid unofficially."

"I do. What's happened?"

"King Sajjid asked Mr. Bemis to bring over a favorite niece of his. She's nineteen and there's been a delay about her admittance."

"Doesn't she have a passport?"

"She has a royal *passe-partout*, signed personally by her uncle. She's been using it for traveling to and from school in Switzerland, but it has no American visa."

"Is that all that's disturbing you?"

"No, sir. A rather excitable woman whom Bemis picked up in Rome is insisting that the girl is actually a slave."

"I beg your pardon?"

"A slave. The charge is absurd, of course, but the Princess has been considerably unnerved by the experience."

"What's been done about it?"

"I've satisfied Immigration the Princess is *extra legam* under the anti-slavery laws."

"Why?"

"The laws apply only to instances of involuntary servitude. The Princess has declared she is here on her own volition."

"A nice point. Have you smoothed her feathers?"

"I think the situation is fairly well in hand, sir. They've let me take her to the private Port Authority lounge where she'll be comfortable until Washington confirms my entry request."

"Are you with her now?"

"No, sir. I'm in the airport infirmary with the woman. They're trying to calm her down."

"Is Bemis there, too?"

"No, sir. He and his fiancée are with the Princess."

"His fiancée? Was she on the plane, too?"

"No, sir. She came up with me from Washington. She's Senator McGravey's daughter, Rowena."

"Oh, yes. Very pretty girl. Anything else?"

"Well, yes, sir." Webster weighed every word. "The Princess has been a bit impatient, and because of the possible effect of the incident on King Sajjid I thought you might wish to . . ."

"You're quite right, Harris. Hold the fort. I'll nip over."

The Secretary addressed the Ambassador. "A very small brush fire at Kennedy. Is there a helicopter handy?"

As Mrs. Wisser was still shaking, the nurse persuaded her to take a sedative and assured her that the man calling himself Webster Harris was in the doctor's office next door putting through the call to California.

Mrs. Wisser closed her eyes, but opened them as she heard the infirmary door slam. It was Morty. He said OWA could get them on an L.A. plane that left in half an hour. After all Mrs. Wisser had been through, she didn't know whether she should leave on it or not. Why was the call to Azusa taking so long? Another wave of panic swept over her. What if that Harris, instead of getting long distance, was by now halfway to the gang's headquarters?

"Morty, are you absolutely sure that man is from the State Department?"

"Mrs. Wisser, what proof do you need? The government people downstairs were taking his orders, weren't they? What's eating you; you keep being so suspicious?"

"What's eating me, as you call it, should be eating other people. Morty, you are both young and inexperienced and totally blind to what's happening in this country. Why, I could tell you things . . ."

"O.K. Hold it. You want the five thousand bucks?"

"What?"

"If you don't show up in L.A. tomorrow, you can kiss five grand good-bye. No show, no dough. Yes or no? How about using your head?"

Mrs. Wisser tried to think. It was simply terrible to be in such a position. She asked Morty to do just one thing for her—see if that call to Azusa was really being placed. Morty left.

The nurse came over and patted her hand again and told her not to worry about anything. The nurse seemed like a nice girl; of course unaware of what anyone with eyes could read about in fearless magazines like *The American Patrol, Uncle Sam's Defenders,* and *The Death of a Nation.* Facts that showed what the commies and socialists all the way to the Supreme Court and the White House were doing to sell out America. What would this poor girl know about the facts? Until they let her talk to Fred, the wisest thing was to keep mum and trust nobody.

"O.K., Mrs. Wisser." Morty was calling from the doorway. "Can you get up? Your husband's on the line."

Mrs. Wisser found the strength to rise. In the doctor's office, the man who called himself Harris hadn't left after all and was at the telephone.

"Here she is now, Mr. Wisser," she heard him say into it.

Still alert to villainy, she accepted the receiver and mustered strength to speak.

"Hello?"

"Madge?" Her heart leaped—it was Fred's voice!

"Oh, Fred, honey. How are you?"

"I'll tell you when you get here. They say you can leave in half an hour. I'll meet the plane."

"Oh, Fred, you don't know what I've been through. I'm in such a state."

"Madge."

"Yes, Fred?"

"Shut up, honey. I know all about what's happened. Can you hear me?"

"Yes, Fred."

"Now, listen and don't talk. Just quietly get on that plane and be glad you're not in jail."

"I beg your pardon?"

"In jail—as a public nuisance. You've meddled in something you don't know anything about. Are there people around you?"

"Yes, there are."

"Then keep quiet and let me finish."

"But I don't understand what you mean by . . ."

"Don't try to. I'm telling you to listen. Whatever you thought you heard was wrong. The girl is a very important guest of the Department of State and if you keep slandering her you can be in very, very hot water. Did you hear me?"

"Yes, Fred."

"So don't talk any more to anybody and get on that plane. Is that clear?"

"Yes, Fred. But, listen Fred . . . Fred . . . ?" Fred had hung up.

"O.K. Good-bye, dear," said Mrs. Wisser for the sake of appearances. Maybe Fred was at the bank and didn't want to talk any more because somebody there might hear him. It was hard to see what she'd done wrong, but Fred would tell her when he got over his mad. In the meantime she would naturally watch her step.

"All set?" asked Morty.

"All set."

"They'll put us on board whenever you're ready."

"I'm ready."

Mrs. Wisser, world traveler and patriot, had decided just to think about the five thousand dollars. She was even able to smile a little at the OWA man as he showed her and Morty to the plane.

Rowena's composure was being severely strained. She had come to New York, anticipating a quiet discussion during which, with Webster's skillful help, Newton would be made to see that his naïveté in money matters could not be tolerated. For almost an hour she had been unable to exchange more than ten words with him because of the flood of embarrassments for which he alone was responsible. However inspired he might be in his laboratory, he could certainly be stupid when faced with everyday responsibilities. Why hadn't he used his brains to tell people that the Suruki Embassy woman would not be with him on the plane and that he was escorting a bewildered young thing from Sajjid's palace instead? Had he assumed the substitution would cause no more concern than a change of bridge partners? And then, inviting a wormy press-agent photographer and a moronic harridan to come along, too! What a fine mess it would have been if Webster hadn't been there to bring the Immigration people to their senses. Who was Webster talking to at that telephone? The girl seemed still shaken by her experience downstairs. The Secretary apparently wasn't making much progress trying to put her at her ease.

Rowena watched Webster hang up the phone, and speak privately to the Secretary. Then the assuasions to the girl were resumed. Why did Newton think his presence was necessary?

As if her thoughts had reached him, Newton looked over to where Rowena was sitting. He came to her side.

"I'm terribly sorry, dear, but Farha has been rather shaken up. She doesn't quite know what she wants to do."

"You said she was going to stay with the Suruki Ambassador and his wife."

"Yes, I did." Newton hesitated. "I said it to help Webster with the passport examiners. Actually she doesn't want to go to Washington."

"Why doesn't she?" What was giving Newton such mental difficulties? Whenever he raked his hair like that you knew his mind was racing to decide something.

"I've had no chance to tell you, dear, but Farha is not simply a visitor. In a way she is my personal guest."

"Your 'guest?' " What new imbecility had he committed? "You invited her?"

Across the room he saw Farha nervously talking with the Secretary.

"Look at me, please. You're fidgeting even more than when they made that man take the film out of his camera."

"I'm sorry. The fact is the Suruki Embassy didn't know the Princess was coming. They're trying to reach Dr. Hunain now at a cocktail party. In the meantime the Secretary is trying to persuade Farha to let him take her and the rest of us to dinner."

"It's becoming quite a party, isn't it?"

"Rowena, I'm sorry this delay is so irksome, but I'm afraid I can't do much about it."

"Don't give it a thought, dear. When you learn whether or not the Ambassador is joining us, too, you might cancel the reservation Webster made for the three of us at the Voisin. In the meantime it would be interesting to learn why that little number happens to be your guest."

"I've been wanting to tell you and I'll be glad to if you will stop looking at me as though you were sighting a rifle."

"Please go ahead," invited Rowena without lowering her aim.

An embittered Rowena was new and disconcerting. Yet, Newton told himself, he must not allow her irritation to affect his own emotions. What was important at the moment was that she be informed of the facts.

"If you can be patient, Rowena, I can set your mind at rest. Saying Farha is my guest merely indicates how I regard her. Actually, she is a gift."

"A gift?"

"A gift. King Sajjid happens to be a wildly eccentric, overly generous man. He convinced himself that the only present I might be willing to accept from him was Farha." Newton looked vainly for an indication of the amusement he had expected his embarrassment would provide.

"So that insane woman's story was true."

"Of course not. She thought it was true, I suppose. She did overhear Farha telling me why her uncle thought I'd take her."

"I see. And why did he?"

"She had done some secretarial work for me."

"Fancy that. I wouldn't have ever guessed your little keepsake was an office worker."

"I'm serious, Rowena. She knows you and I are engaged. She imagined she might become part of our household. It's fantastic, I'll admit, but then everything that's happened to me in the last forty-eight hours has been fantastic. I've been moving about in a sort of pageant of implausibilities. I let myself believe you would laugh with me about it."

"Perhaps I'll find it hilarious later. At the moment I'm trying not to chuckle at something else. Did you sleep with her?"

"Rowena!"

"I wouldn't call that an answer, dear."

"Is that what's been disturbing you?"

"Oh, no. It's just interesting to recall that until we drove to Williamsburg you said you were a virgin."

"Goddamn it, I was!"

"Mr. Bemis!" The Secretary seldom raised his voice. To gain Newton's attention he had raised it only slightly. But Webster's blood chilled. He noted the slow precision familiar to subordinates being hauled on the carpet. He had first witnessed it at a departmental meeting following a disclosure in the press of a restricted intelligence item. On that occasion Webster had watched senior colleagues quail facing the Secretary's quiet, Borean comments. Although gratefully aware that he was blameless in the present crisis, Webster clasped his hands firmly behind his back to maintain his imperturbability.

Newton, wrenched from his unexpected and harrowing exchange of confidences with Rowena, was equally unprepared for either the grimness of the Secretary or the sight of Farha, collapsed in an overstuffed chair and sobbing her heart out.

"I have been speaking on the telephone," said the Secretary, "with King Sajjid's ambassador in Washington. He read me a cable he has received from Suruk. If you aided Princess Farha's unauthorized departure, you will have done a grave disservice to your country."

Webster's toes were curling when the point of Newton's approaching nose stopped within an inch of the Secretary's.

"I'd like to know what you're so crusty about."

Farha came from her chair, trembling.

"Wait, Mr. Bemis!" She faced the Secretary. "You cannot blame Mr. Bemis. I lied to him. I told him I was a gift from my uncle. Mr. Bemis, I tricked you. It was a terrible thing to do, but it offered my only chance to escape an intolerable situation. I did not dare tell you I was running away lest you inform my uncle."

"Is it true you were hoodwinked?" questioned the Secretary. Newton was looking at a Farha he hadn't believed existed.

"I'll tell you when I stop spinning."

Farha resumed.

"I am telling the truth. My grandmother—you knew her as Mrs. Haruba—helped me. She told me to hide in the plane until it left Rome." Farha turned to the Secretary. At the moment, the exoneration of Mr. Bemis was more important than her own calamity. "Is it clear now that Mr. Bemis had nothing to do with my coming?"

"Is her story correct?"

Newton intended to supplement his nod with speech, but the Secretary gave him no time to find words.

"Get me through to Professor Drench," he ordered.

Webster had his hands unlocked in time to pick up the telephone receiver.

"May I join this little gathering?" Rowena asked brightly. "One gets lonely being out of things." Her words were directed at the Secretary, but Newton could feel a bayonet's point.

"There's been a misunderstanding," said Newton, firmly. "It can be cleared up if you will go and sit down again."

"I beg your pardon?" said Rowena from one of the loftier reaches of Mount Everest.

"I said, sit down," Newton resounded from an adjacent height. The Secretary could not allow the situation to be worsened by a lovers' brouhaha.

"Miss McGravey!" The Secretary's feet were on lower ground, but Rowena heard and responded to the authority in his voice.

"What?"

"I wish to tell you something, privately. Excuse us, Your Highness." Still dazed by Newton's unpardonable discourtesy, Rowena permitted herself to be led away.

Newton's Attendant Realist, after drowsing for too long a period, was alert and prodding.

So Farha is a pathetic invertebrate, so psychologically shackled to the degraded status of Muslim females it would be impossible for her to want freedom. You're quite a student of character, aren't you?

I made a mistake.

I'll say you did. And speaking of freedom, now that a few scales have dropped from your eyes, why not take a good look at Rowena. She couldn't be emancipated from her own kind of slavery if she lived a thousand years. Isn't it time for you to recognize her addiction to externalities: elaborate weddings, big town houses, and the aggrandizing of charming, unpretentious country ones? You've wasted a lot of time shoring up that pedestal you've kept her on. Why didn't you try looking at her on the ground? Was it because your rudimentary brain couldn't stop worshipping her?

I assumed she was entitled to extra admiration because she was so beautiful.

It was gratuitous. Should there be a contest for Miss Galactic System she has hundreds of photographs ready for submission. And God help the judges who didn't crown her queen of the heavens.

And whatever prompted you to believe groveling was the only curative treatment for tantrums? I might have stayed asleep if I hadn't heard you begging her to withhold judgment on your misad-

venture. Now, perhaps, you see she has the same spirit of forbear-
ance as a hawk in a henyard. And while I have your ear, what about
your whipping up all those damn fool excuses for her pretensions
to scientific knowledge? Where's the man who said he would stop
being a booby about women?

Right here. What about this girl?

Find out for yourself. I hope I'll be around if you need me.

"Are you too angry to speak to me, Mr. Bemis?"

"I beg your pardon. I hadn't realized you were so courageous,"
he smiled. "And I'd never have guessed I could be taken in so completely." His thoughts went to her artful story on the plane. "When
did you find out I played chess?"

"You told me so when you unwrapped Uncle Sajjid's set."

"Didn't you bring it so that our playing would keep me from
asking too many questions?"

"Oh, no, Mr. Bemis. When I came to the airport at Qam, the
stewardess told me she had a package for you. I said I would deliver
it, so she gave it to me. It really was from my uncle."

Webster left the receiver uncradled and joined the Secretary.

"Professor Drench is coming to the phone, sir."

"Good. Miss McGravey would like to wait downstairs for you."

"I'll be in the Alitalia lounge, Webster darling."

"Right." Webster hurried back to the telephone.

Eyeing the Secretary's return, Newton did not notice Rowena's
exit.

"If I can help the Princess in any way, I want to do it."

"At the moment," said the Secretary, "I suggest that you stand
by. I might ask you to tell Professor Drench how the Princess
tricked you."

"Here he is, sir," reported Webster.

The Secretary gave a final word to Newton. "It may not be easy
to regain His Majesty's friendship." He put the receiver to his ear
and initiated apologetic greetings in governmentese. Farha had

stopped crying. Mr. Bemis' sympathy had made her feel slightly less desperate.

"I don't know how the law operates," said Newton, "but maybe we can get you asylum here as a political refugee."

"If I were allowed to stay my uncle would never forgive your country. The Secretary of State has said he wants my uncle's good will, so I expect I will be sent home."

Webster touched Newton's shoulder and pointed to the Secretary. The latter was beckoning Newton.

"Here is Mr. Bemis, Professor Drench. He will corroborate what I have told you." Newton was given the receiver.

"Hello, Professor Drench."

"Hello, Mr. Bemis. His Majesty—wait a moment, please."

"Tell the filthy dog," shouted Abdel Sadek, "that I will come to America and kill him."

"If you do not stop screaming, I cannot hear the American," Drench complained. The fury of Abdel Sadek did not lessen. He considered snatching the telephone from Drench, but as his English was even less fluent than Sajjid's he elaborated his intentions in colorful and explicit Arabic.

"Restrain yourself, my friend," demanded Sajjid. "Remember I have been offended as much as you."

"We are having a discussion, Mr. Bemis," said Drench, "which I hope will soon be finished."

"Let me speak to him, my uncle," said Sajjid. "Misser Bemis?" Newton recognized the voice. "Yes."

"Misser Bemis, why you go doing so wrong a thing? I did thought you were a friend of me and most trusting-worth man."

"And I thought you were a man with decent instincts!"

When necessary the Secretary could spring to action.

"Give me that!" Having wrested the telephone away, he applied diplomatic oil with lightning speed. "Professor Drench, the outrageous insult you heard was uttered irresponsibly and, I assure you, completely misrepresents the deep respect and high regard with which my government—"

"Wait!" Sajjid interjected. "Much of noises here, Misser Bemis. Speaking more loud and not be so fast. You thought I were what man?"

The Secretary stiffened, put his hand over the mouthpiece and wheeled to Bemis.

"Whom were you talking to?" he whispered.

"The King."

One of the reasons for the Secretary's appointment was his ability to swim calmly through boiling water. He uncovered the receiver.

"Your Majesty."

"Misser Bemis, you do hear me say I did thought you were a friend of me." Another voice, harsh and insistent, was making Sajjid's inaudible. The Secretary waited patiently. Suddenly he heard "Wait, Misser Bemis! *Hene khod, 'amm* Wex!" Then an English voice reached his ear.

"Are you there, Mr. Bemis?"

"This is not Bemis. Who is speaking, please?"

"Wexford Drench here."

"Ah, Professor Drench. This is the Secretary again. As I was trying to tell you—"

"One moment, sir. There's rather a disturbance here. Could you possibly stand by?"

"Of course, Professor." The Secretary listened for half a minute to a distant cacophony. He offered the receiver to Webster. "Let me know when they're back on."

There was no indication of the Secretary's mental dishevelment as he extracted a cigarette from its case and placidly put it in his mouth. In the nick of time he withdrew his lighter from the filter end. He turned to Farha and Newton.

"Fortunately, His Majesty seems not to have heard you. I don't know what prompted your rashness, but—Yes, Harris?"

"Nothing, sir. I thought they were back on the line. It was just louder Arabic."

In the King's study, Abdel Sadek was struggling vainly against the two guards Sajjid had summoned. He could not move his arms and legs, but he was still ungagged. With unabated vehemence he varied only slightly the demands which Sajjid was declining to have Drench translate into English.

"And if the leprous dog is not in our hands within twenty-four hours, their filthy ambassador will be nailed to the House of the Spike and when the oil wells are taken away from the cheating ASOCO criminals and—"

The newly arrived chief *mlazim* of the palace police placed his hands firmly over Abdel Sadek's mouth.

"Whether you wish to hear or not," said Sajjid, "you will listen to what Professor Drench will translate to the American statesman. You were unwise to insist that the oil leases be given to the Russians. It confirmed several hints that have been made recently of your duplicity. All the sympathy I felt for you at first has been replaced by joyousness because a terrified girl has escaped a lying traitor. Uncle Wex, will you tell Mr. Bemis that I am very grateful that he aided the Lady Farha and ask him to give her shelter until she decides to come home?"

"I must say I am relieved, Mr. Bemis," the Secretary conceded. "It is odd that His Majesty's message to Dr. Hunain was misconstrued, but those things happen sometimes."

The Secretary's eyes went to Farha. "Do you know any Arabic, Mr. Bemis?"

"Not enough to know what she's saying to the King."

When Farha left the telephone she was crying again, this time because she was so happy.

"Uncle Sajjid finds it hard to believe that you did not help my grandmother with her scheme. Nevertheless, he feels more in debt to you than ever. Tonight I am to telephone him about something that concerns him greatly."

"What's that?" asked Newton.

"He hopes you are going to keep the chess set."

Chapter 18

Farha's visit with Tabby Proctor, to whom she had vaguely planned to flee after arriving in New York, lasted eight weeks.

"Why must you go to Washington?" argued Tabby's mother. "Let me write to your grandmother and ask her to join you here. We would be delighted to have her, and Tabby has dozens more young friends you haven't met yet."

"I'm sure Grandmother would love to visit Kentucky, and perhaps later she can come back with me, but if I am to enter Columbia, I must go to New York next week. Grandmother and someone from the embassy are going to come with me."

Newton had found it surprisingly easy to recover from Rowena's severance of their engagement. Yet as the months went by certain phrases in her *congé* letter still grated when he thought about them.

I might as well tell you that the advisability of sending you on your way had occurred to me even before you revealed yourself so vividly at the airport. Until then I had foolishly hoped you could be taught to acquire a more adult point of view about money. If it hadn't been for that hypocritical puzzled-little-boy expression on your face while trying to justify the presence of that Arabian cooky, I might have continued to believe I had become involved with a half-witted cub scout, not quite old enough to be trusted out of doors.

One night in October as Newton got out of the taxi at his flat, Timmy asked if he could come up a moment before going on to his own. While Newton mixed nightcaps, Timmy sorted the thoughts that had been disturbing him since dinner.

"Yes, I do have something on my mind. I was watching you all evening. Have you ever considered having your head examined by a competent authority?"

"Is there a pressing need for it?"

"I'm inclined to think so. Part of your brain doesn't seem to function at all. I refer to the romance sector."

"You've heard me say exactly how I feel."

"About Rowena, yes. I am thinking of a girl who makes Rowena look like one of the homelier females in Endor."

"Are you talking about Farha?"

"God, you're sharp tonight. That's exactly who I had in mind. What in hell's the matter with you?"

"You mean about being in love with her?"

"Yes," snapped Timmy.

"She's just a kid. Anyway, she's talking about Sajjid finding her a suitable husband; probably, the son he's picked as his heir. He's her second cousin and she says he's a fine boy."

"Then why is she so delighted to be living in America and studying at Columbia? Why does she throw off rainbows every time she looks at you? For God's sake have you never thought of her as desirable?"

"Of course I have. I found her attractive the night I met her."

"You told me you never saw her until she showed up on the plane."

"That's true. It was when we were in one of those unbelievable gardens. She had that wicker thing over her head, but I noticed her ankles and feet. Later I wondered why I'd once been concerned with eugenic engineering."

"Then, wake up, you utterly incredible dope!"

After Timmy went home Newton's Attendant Realist gave him a lacing he was never to forget.

"I know you close in five minutes," said Newton, "but my other witness should be here momentarily." He spoke to Farha. "Timmy's seldom late and he's bright enough to find his way to the marriage bureau."

Farha was serenely undisturbed. It was impossible to be any happier—Newton seated on one side of her, holding her hand, and Grandmother, more sedate but no less contented, on the other. The marriage clerk assured Newton it was no trouble at all to wait. Before they arrived, he had been told the identity of the principals and being a bachelor himself was wondering how much more it would cost if, instead of going tourist to Paris next Spring, he went to Suruk. If one ordinary looking American could catch himself a dish like this, maybe he might get a wonderful break too.

"I have another reason for believing it will be a successful marriage," said the Princess Budur. "You, my dear boy, have a great deal of your being in the future. And part of Farha is still lingering in the long-ago. I think you will both have a happy adventure sharing today."

"I'm sorry we're late," said Timmy, "but we had to take a taxi. His Majesty's car must have got lost in the traffic somewhere."

"Is my fault entirety," said Sajjid. "I did tell him to come for Misser Thackaray and me to Eas' Fiffity-four Street. The lawyer office is on Wes' Fiffity-four Street."

"How did you make out?"

"Everything bonzo," said Sajjid. He gave his imminent nephew an avuncular hug. "The Paragon Drug Store in Drayton—"

"Dayton," corrected Timmy.

"Dayton, Ohio. Misser Thackaray do buy it in his name. In two month my English—you see I do not to say Engliss anymore—will going be even better as now.

"So now we have wedding. O.K., Misser Bemis?"

KBIR PALACE
QAM
1965